OAKWOOD

David Jones

ISBN:978-1-9193251-1-8

Dedicated to all those who have made mistakes, realised them, and tried, however unsuccessfully, to rectify them.

THE YIELDING

They said it couldn't happen.
Then, it happened quickly.
It only took fifty years.

The rising sea level had brought havoc.

Humanity had yielded to the oceans, and in that calamity, everything else yielded to the inevitable chaos of a fading civilisation.

Part 1

1

The father tentatively went outside.

There was no sign of the drone swarm. Almost every window in every cottage in the village of Oakwood was smashed. There was a scattering of bodies outside some of the cottages, and weeping relatives hunched over the bloodied bodies.

He caught sight of a group of three men entering the village from the north side. They were not of the village, and they walked with an air of confidence. They were all armed. The father turned and ran past two or three of the houses to his left, in full view of the three men. He went inside and exited via the rear. He doubled back, hoping not to be seen, to his house and family.

"We must leave now! Leave everything," the father said.

"What's happening? Oh God, what's happening!" shouted the mother.

"Never mind. Come on. Now! Or it will be too late."

The parents gathered up the boys and headed for the back door.

The door to the small farmhouse opened, and two of the three men strode in with their guns displayed for effect. The third man had gone to the back door, cutting off any hope of an escape. The householders had not managed to escape the farmhouse before the intruders arrived.

The third man made his way through the house and rejoined his coworkers.

"No drones came here! We need to rework their programming, I think. But anyway, nothing wrong with the personal touch now and then," said the lead man.

He smiled at the family. The smile was broader on one side of his face than the other. The man took a seat in the armchair next to the fire, resting his gun on his lap. He nodded at his standing colleagues. The nonverbal message was immediately understood and acted upon, and the householders soon found themselves tied up with bits of rope that the men seemed to magic up from nowhere. The mother was screaming, and the father was yelling, "No! No! No!" The man sitting in the chair with the gun across his lap continued to grin.

The mother was dragged to one of the bedrooms, and the screaming stopped.

The men went into the bedroom in turns.

There was a gunshot from the bedroom, and the last man came out and turned to the father and the boys. His smile was slightly off-centre, a combination of a prominent canine tooth and a slight droop of the eyelid on the left side. He ran a hand through his red hair. He looked deep in thought as he lifted his gun and shot the father in the chest. He smiled at the boys. Then he turned for the door and left without a backwards glance.

The father desperately crawled over to the boys. He was ghostly white with a crimson-red stain spreading across his chest. He managed to untie his elder son, who quickly freed the younger. Both boys bent over their now slumped father.

* * *

Blood was dripping from the corner of his mouth now. "Head north." He whispered. "Find the river. Follow it to the sea. Find the big city. You will find what you need."

He smiled at both the boys and closed his eyes.

2

Myra Kraxler liked to escape. She liked to escape from whatever she felt was confining her. Sometimes, it was her house, her lovely house. Sometimes, it was her children, her lovely children. Sometimes, it was the servants, the lovely servants. Sometimes, it was her husband, Kelvin.

She could not always tell the origin of her feelings, but the result was almost always the same: leave, if only for a short time.

Myra sat on the balcony of her house, looking out at the sea. The house wouldn't have been close to the sea one hundred years ago. It was a modern house that resembled a structure made from giant white cubes randomly stacked on top of each other. A lot of glass allowed the sea views to enter and fill the insides with natural light. It was not a cheap house, set as it was on the waterfront of the most upmarket part of the city of Tangreco. She could see her three children playing on their private beach, supervised by Samantha Keogh, the live-in nanny.

Sam was in her mid-twenties and slim of figure, topped with a mop of auburn hair that just failed to make it to ginger. It fell over her shoulders in gentle curls, framing her face and naturally gentle smile. Samantha and her husband Elliott had been the live-in servants for the past five years. They had no defined duties, but over time, Sam had gravitated towards Myra and Elliott towards Kelvin.

Myra rose from her seat and strode down the steps to the beach.

"Sam."

"Oh. Hi Myra. What's up?"

"Could you throw some things into a bag for the kids? I think I will take them to Mother's place for a day or two."

"Uh, okay. What's up?"

"Nothing. It's just they haven't been over for a while."

"Shall I call Elliott to come and drive you? I think he's in the office in town with Kelvin."

"No. I'll drive myself."

"You know Kelvin won't like that. Not with how things are going in the city."

"It'll be fine. Half an hour, okay?"

"Um—"

"Good," Myra said, closing the door on further discussion.

She could see a hint of sadness in Sam's face. It was a sadness that had gradually grown over the time they had lived at the house. The corners of her eyes told of much laughter. The giveaway creases were always there. But increasingly, those creases seemed to be dormant unless she was playing with the children. Sam seemed to come fully alive around the children. Myra was becoming increasingly convinced that the inner sadness she felt in Sam was, at least in part, due to her not having children of her own.

"Go grab some stuff. We are off to Granny's. Sienna, help Leon and Connie get some things while Sam packs the essentials. See you all at the car in half an hour." Myra turned and ran up the steps to the house to pack herself.

By the time Sam brought the children out to the front of the house, Myra was already in the car, engine running. Her rucksack lay on the passenger seat. Sam strapped Sienna, Leon, and Connie into the back seat, hugging each in turn before shutting the door. She stepped back to speak to Myra through her open window.

"Shall—"

"No, don't tell them I've gone without anyone. They will get too cross, and the whole thing will end in tears. Better to let them calm down. They can come and fetch me in a day or two."

"Cross is the wrong word. Furious, more like."

"Bye." Myra set the car on course for the main gate and the road beyond. She just caught a glimpse of the empty sadness in Sam's face before she turned away.

"She will have called Elliott within ten minutes, and he will instantly tell Kelvin. I'll be away by then, though," thought Myra.

Myra drove through the city without stopping. There was less and less motor traffic in the city over the last few years. What little there was did not like stopping en route. It was good to keep the envious looks at bay, at a distance, and as fleeting as possible. Everyone ignored the old traffic controls, as if from another age. Having a car meant having wealth, and having wealth these days was a rare commodity. It could also make you a target.

Isabella's house was the antithesis of the Kraxler residence. It was neither modern nor minimalist, and it was situated on the other side of the city, in the foothills of the mountains, far from the sea. The driveway was of small terracotta tiles and led up to a stone archway, over which stretched some of the first-floor accommodation. Through the archway was an enclosed quadrangle containing a mature garden. Surrounding the estate was a high wall enclosing outbuildings, all of which were constructed from the same stone as the main house. There was an inner wall containing an archway identical to the outer one, but offset to obscure the inner house from view. When Myra reached Isabella's place, she drove in through the first arch and turned immediately left, then right, and stopped the car in front of the stone double garage, which was set apart and to the left of the house.

"Come on, you lot. Let's go and see Granny."

Her three children, Sienna, Leon, and Connie, evacuated the car and went to the trunk. It was a well-trodden path. Myra pinged the trunk open, and the children grabbed their stuff. Myra's rucksack remained untouched on the front seat. The whole tribe headed for the inner arch into the garden.

"Mum," called Myra.

"Hi, My," came the reply from somewhere amongst the greenery.

"I've brought the kids to see you."

"Nice. Are you staying too?"

"No, sorry. I need some mountain."

"Stay a while. Have tea or coffee. Half an hour? Come on, Myra."

Her mum was the only person she could put up with, shortening her name to "My". Everyone else was put right on the matter very sharply. What her mother called her was a useful barometer, too. "My" was good, but "Myra" meant she was on shaky ground and that she needed to tread carefully.

"A coffee would be nice while the kids play in the garden. Are you okay to have them for a bit?"

Back on solid "My" territory now.

"Yes, of course. Let's go make the coffee."

Sienna, Leon, and Connie were uninterested in coffee or the garden and ran off to explore the stone outbuildings. Sienna played with some of her grandmother's terracotta pots.

Isabella busied herself with coffee-making, while Myra fussed about looking for something to receive the brown brew once it was made.

"Need more mountain, eh?" asked Isabella.

"Just escaping."

"From what, Myra?"

"You know what I'm like. I need space sometimes."

"From your husband?"

"I never see him. He's always at work. With Elliott in tow."

"Someone has to keep the family finances on an even keel," Isabella said.

Coffee poured into cups.

"I know. It's just that the world has gone a bit mad lately. Life is good because we are well off, but almost everywhere you look, there seem to be people with almost nothing, and the gap between us is growing. I hate it, but there is nothing to be done. Except escape to the mountains or the sea, now and then."

"Maybe all generations feel that the world has changed for the worse during their occupancy of it."

"Maybe," considered Myra.

"And maybe we have just been lucky until now. Either way, we just have to get on with it and make thanks for the good times."

Both put their cups down on the kitchen table at the same time, neither having drunk from them. It naturally brought the chat to a close. As if choreographed, they both rose from their chairs together and smiled at one another.

"How long will you be gone?"

"Just a day or two. Are you good to have the little monsters till I get back?"

"They are only monsters for you. They are always angels for me."

"Because you spoil them."

"True. Leave them here for a couple of days of spoiling, then. And be careful in the mountains."

"I will."

"Come on. Let's get the goodbyes done so I can return to tending the garden and spoiling your offspring."

"Thanks, Mum. I love you."

They hugged. Then headed to the garden to find the children.

Having found them, Myra hugged the kids in turn.

"Group hug!" Shouted Sienna.

They all indulged.

Myra turned, grabbed her backpack, and trotted out of the house, heading for the hills.

3

Carlos screamed, shattering the misty silence of the forest floor. Victor leaned across and comforted his shaking younger brother. "It's okay, Carlos," he said, hugging him close.

"No, it isn't. It will never be okay."

Victor hugged Carlos more tightly. It had become a morning routine. Carlos's dreamed recollection of the day that everything changed. Then came the screams, followed by consoling hugs from his brother.

"Father told us what to do," Victor said.

"I know, but he didn't tell us how to do it before…"

"He told us to head north, find the river and follow it to the sea. He told us to find the big city."

"And then what?"

"We will find what we need."

"I need some food. I'm starving."

"Yeah, we both are. Just stay still for a while, and then we will carry on with what Father told us to do."

Carlos, almost whispering to himself, said, "It will never be okay."

"I will make it okay," encouraged Victor. And he thought, *"But it will never be the same."*

Both boys closed their eyes and lay silently on the forest

floor, each inevitably recalling the events that had brought them here.

Ten days ago, the men with guns came to the village and told the villagers they must all leave. Victor replayed it in his head.

"Leave before seven days are up. Take what you like, but leave. If you are here when we come back, you will stay here forever. In a box under the ground. If we can be bothered with boxes or digging."

All the families of Oakwood met that night to settle upon what to do. Most started packing their belongings to head south, away from the direction from which the men with guns had come. Father had disagreed.

"We have put too much effort into our farms to leave them, to have them stolen from us. We should, we must stay!"

Some decided to stay, and some chose to leave. The Atkar family stayed, and the men came back. Three men.

The two young boys buried their parents in the back garden of their farmhouse.

Carlos said, "You're shaking."

"I'm just cold and shivering. Come on. Let's see if we can find our way to some food and warmth," Victor said.

"I'm tired and want to go home!" exclaimed Carlos.

"Carlos, we don't have a home anymore. We just have each other. I have you, and you have me. That's it. We must look out for one another. Come on. It will be fine, you'll see."

The boys got to their feet and reluctantly shouldered their little backpacks, which Victor had packed. Victor grabbed Carlos's left hand and gave it an encouraging squeeze. His other hand delved into the pocket of his shorts. It retrieved an old-fashioned compass—a family heirloom from generations ago. Victor had grabbed it, along with some other things, from the house after the men with guns had gone. Father had taught them how to use it.

They headed north through the fir trees. Pine needles softened their footsteps so that only the occasional crack of a fallen twig or branch joined the avian dawn chorus. Mist swirled through the branches above them.

"It's getting lighter. I think the mist is lifting, and the sun is coming up," encouraged Victor.

"Are the trees getting more gappy?" asked Carlos.

"I think they are. Come on. Let's keep going for a bit. We might get some sun on us to warm us up. Then we can stop and have a look to see if we got any food left in our backpacks."

Victor's prediction turned out to be accurate. Half an hour later, they had emerged from the trees onto a grassy outlook populated by limestone boulders. The sun was winning the battle with the remaining wisps of mist. They stopped and rested on one of the boulders and searched their backpacks for anything that could be described as breakfast. They were forced to make the best of some stale bread and cheese.

"You know I don't like cheese," said Carlos, disappointedly.

"I know. You choose then. Bread or cheese?"

Carlos squeezed the rock-hard bread and chose the cheese. Victor reclaimed it and divided it a little more fairly. It was gone in a flash, and they both lay back on the rock to rest.

Revived, they set off again.

"Can you hear that?" said Victor.

"What?"

"I think I can hear water. Over there." Victor pointed to their left. "Come on. Father said to find the river."

They were too tired to run, but they picked up the pace

and headed towards the sound of the water. Soon, they reached it, or at least the path that ran alongside it. The river was milky in colour, slow-flowing and very wide.

"Oh," said Victor

"What?"

"The sound of water isn't coming from the river. It's coming from there." Victor pointed downstream.

"The mist has come back," said Carlos.

"I think the mist never goes from here. Father said to follow the river to the sea. We need to go that way." Victor pointed towards the swirling mists.

The boys followed the riverside path towards the mist. The noise eventually grew to a roar. The path widened as it passed the torrent, allowing them to stop and take in the vista of the falls. The water tumbled off a large arrowhead of rock into a churning, boiling pool below. Mists swirled around them, alternately clearing and obscuring their view of the falls and the river below.

"We're not going to jump…are we?" asked Carlos.

"We must follow the river and get down there."

"I'm not jumping," exclaimed Carlos, backing away.

"No, we are not jumping. There must be another way."

They sat silently for a while until they became so saturated with the waterfall's mists that they had to move.

"Let's stick to the path. It must go somewhere." Victor explained

"Good idea. But will you lead the way?"

"Of course I will." Victor clasped his brother's hand again.

The path led on, veering away from the falls slightly and started a gentle descent towards what looked like an opening to a cave. When the boys reached it, they could see that it was a rectangular tunnel cut into the rock. It was wide enough to allow three sizable adults to walk through it side by side with ease. The walls were lined with moss, and the tunnel floor was shiny and slippery. The boys entered the tunnel, and Victor encouraged Carlos to follow. "Come on. There's light at the end, then it's just a path again."

The path became drier inside the tunnel, and the boys headed on. Ahead of them, the left-hand tunnel wall had collapsed, opening up a view into the gorge on their left, leaving the path bounded by rock above, below and to the right. It also made the path narrower. The missing tunnel wall allowed access to the mists, making the foothold on the downward-sloping gouge in the cliff face treacherous. There was a rusty metal railing on the outer edge of the path, but it was so in need of repair that whole sections of it were missing. A more modern-looking steel wire handhold ran along the inner wall and was attached to the wall at intervals.

"Hold on to this," said Victor. "Don't use the rail. It's not safe."

They eventually made it safely down to river level. It had taken most of the day. Hunger and fatigue hit them again. They drank from the milky river waters and finished the dry bread. Both took off their shoes and cooled their feet in the waters.

"Now we need to find somewhere to sleep for the night. I think we have had enough walking for today, but we will need to do a bit more, little brother," said Victor.

Carlos said nothing in reply, just sitting at the water's edge, watching his feet.

"Come on. Let's walk a bit further along the river and see if we can find somewhere to sleep."

Carlos gave in silently and followed his older brother along the path, holding his hand for comfort.

4

The top floor of the new Kraxler building was a combination of office and apartment. The whole top floor was designed to slowly rotate, so that the view constantly changed. It was a real indulgence, given how bad things were generally in the city and beyond. But it was a symbol of his wealth and power, and Kelvin thought it wise to make both of those things highly visible to the inhabitants of Tangreco. Kelvin loved it here, but Myra was not so keen. She preferred the family house. She was not someone to flaunt things to other people either. As a result, she was a rare visitor.

Access to the apartment was by elevator and was restricted to a small cohort of family, close friends and a few trusted servants. Everyone else had to be admitted by someone already in the apartment or by security. The elevator opened onto a circular anteroom, off which were six separate doors to the Kraxler inner sanctum. Each had a small but discrete label to indicate what lay behind, as, given the whole thing rotated, it was impossible to be sure what lay behind each door.

The day at street level was dull, brought on by a low mist that had rolled in from the sea. Kelvin didn't mind. He was only ten stories up, but he found himself above the mist, and the sun shone brightly in. He felt fantastic. He wasn't worried that Myra had gone off to see her mother in the south of the city. He wasn't worried that the children were not around. Kelvin soaked up the peace and poured himself a stiff drink, which he sipped slowly.

As the alcohol slowly soaked into his system, Kelvin seemed to swell with pride and self-importance. He sat in his favourite chair, taking in the view of the misty city below him and letting himself be warmed by the sunshine. He looked around his apartment, which doubled as an office. Everything was set out as he wanted it.

At last, I've made it. All those years of hard work and manoeuvring finally paid off. No more than I deserve.

5

Exhausted, Victor and Carlos needed to find shelter before darkness fell.

"We must be close to the city now," said Victor. "Tomorrow will be good."

Carlos said nothing. He was beyond speech. Victor continued with a monologue commentary, in an attempt to provide comfort for himself as much as for his little brother.

"It's busier now—more people and more noise. I think we should get off the road in a while so we can sleep and rest. Find some shelter. Tomorrow will be good."

They trudged on for another half hour or so. Carlos was essentially now being dragged along the dirt road into the city. A breeze had picked up, and the day's warmth was ebbing away.

"Let's sit and rest by this wall for a while. Come on. Tomorrow will be good," encouraged Victor.

The boys sat together at the roadside, sheltered from the rising breeze by a dilapidated red brick wall. Carlos rested his head on Victor's shoulder.

"Tomorrow will be good," said Victor.

Again, Carlos said nothing, but he hadn't heard his brother. He was already asleep.

* * *

Myra had left it a bit late to get to her favourite camping spot outside the city. The outskirts would have to do. She would make an early start in the morning. It was time to get off the road and set up the tent before the rising breeze made the task more difficult. She scouted around for a good spot.

Suddenly, she spotted the still forms of two boys huddled in the lee of a small wall. She hurried over and found both asleep. They looked, even whilst asleep, exhausted and hungry. She swung her backpack off and grabbed her phone, trying to get help from Isabella or Sam.

"No service! Again! Phones are pretty unreliable now," she thought.

She left the boys and found a good spot for the tent a little further down the road. She set up the tent and then retraced her steps to where the boys slept.

"Hello." She whispered. Repeating it several times, slightly louder each time.

"What?" Victor jumped, waking Carlos in the process.

"It's okay." Reassured Myra. "Where are your mummy and daddy?"

Carlos started to cry, but Victor managed a weak "We don't have a mummy or daddy."

"Where do you live?"

Victor again. "Nowhere. Here. Nowhere."

"My name is Myra. What are your names?"

Hesitantly, the reply came, "I'm Victor, and this is Carlos."

"Come on, boys. You can't sleep alone on the streets of the city. I will look after you tonight. What do you think? Maybe we could all squeeze into my tent tonight? Tomorrow, we will sort some things out."

The boys just looked at each other and said nothing.

Myra led them to her tent. The boys were grateful for any help from an adult, even a stranger.

"Tomorrow will be good," Victor whispered to Carlos.

6

Stiff and cold. All three of them in the tent were jointly afflicted.

"It's tomorrow," whispered Carlos to Victor without any excitement.

"I know."

"You said tomorrow will be good."

"I know."

"I think it will be boys," assured Myra.

"Come on, let's pack this tent away, and then we can go somewhere I know will be good. Come on."

They packed the tent away and shouldered their backpacks. Last night's breeze had disappeared with the dark, and everything was still.

"Victor. Carlos. We can get a delicious breakfast, but we must walk for about an hour. Okay?"

Both boys nodded and set off, with Myra knowing they would have to wait at least two hours before eating.

"Well-meaning adult deception at its best."

She tried her phone again, just in case there was a signal, but it was a wasted effort.

Encouragement and kind adult company got the boys to two hours into the march.

"There," Myra said, pointing. That big house there. That is where we will have breakfast."

"Is it your house?" said Victor.

"No. My mother lives there. She is a good cook, too."

"What will she cook?" asked a plaintive Carlos.

"We'll see. Something nice, though."

The pace picked up, and they reached the house.

"Come on. My children will be here too."

Myra led them in. In the kitchen, Sienna, Leon and Connie were conversationally silent. This unusual state of affairs was brought about by their mouths being full of waffles.

"Hi, guys. Where's grandma?"

Connie was the first to swallow. "Through there. She is buying a boat."

"What!"

"Yep. A sailing boat."

Myra had no idea what was going on, so she ploughed on and introduced her recent acquisitions.

"Right, guys. This is Victor, and this is Carlos. Carlos and Victor, these are my children. Sienna, Leon and Connie. Can you guys share some of your breakfast, please? We will get some more in a bit. They are starving."

There was a distinct lack of response.

"Now, please!" In a tone that left no doubt that compliance was needed.

"I'm going to see what this boat business is all about."

Myra left the children to fight over the waffles. There was confusion all around. Her children had not expected her back so soon, and definitely not accompanied. Victor and Carlos had never even seen waffles before, and Myra herself found the idea that her mother was buying a sailing boat a little bizarre.

* * *

Myra found Isabella shaking hands with a thin man with a mop of mangled sun-bleached hair.

"Mum?"

"Oh goodness me. You are back quickly. Isabella indicated the man. "This is Jacob," and, indicating Myra, "and this is my daughter."

"Hello, Jacob," said Myra politely. "Are we buying your boat?"

"No, not we. Just your mother."

Myra just looked at the pair of them.

"We are done then," said Jacob.

"Indeed, we are. Thank you for coming. I think it's a win-win deal. Let me show you out."

Myra and the boat people headed through the kitchen to the door.

The children and the waffles were gone.

7

It had taken a year, but now Sam and Elliott Keogh had a brand new house. Purpose-built, in fact, and it served various purposes. Its primary purpose was to house them both, with the addition of Victor and Carlos Atkar, who had been living with the Kraxler family. The move for the boys was not a major upheaval, given that their new residence was immediately adjacent to their old one. Secondarily, the new house allowed Elliott and Kelvin to team up for *work* and Sam and Myra to link up with all five children.

The settling-in process hadn't taken long. Elliott spent most of his time with Kelvin at the Kraxler house, and Sam was relieved to have Myra and all the children in the new house. The arrangement suited them all. However, the adults wished they had made it happen sooner, particularly the women, who felt that the children were growing up too fast and that the new arrangement would quickly become an arrangement of empty nests.

The children of both households were all occupying that challenging and ever-changing zone known as adolescence. The new and fluctuating hormone levels left them and the surrounding adults standing on ever-shifting sands. There was a saving grace, however, in that, like all adolescents, they had an absolute and unshakable belief that they were right and that any to the contrary were utterly wrong. Myra and Sam knew that only time would let these attitudes settle into a more mature outlook. They took comfort in the camaraderie of motherhood, and they took wine, which seemed to help with everything.

8

Kelvin Kraxler once again found himself seated in his favourite chair, looking out over the city as the whole top floor of his office slowly spun around.

His peaceful drink ended when the intercom came to life. Kelvin got up and went over to the keypad and screen.

"Sam Keogh! What are you doing here?" He thought as he poured himself another drink.

"Sam, I thought you had gone to the beach with the kids."

"We did, but the cloud rolled in. They are busy on the climbing wall in your basement, and then they want to go for a swim. Do you want to come down and watch for a bit?"

Kelvin downed his second drink. It burned the back of his throat. It warmed his inside. It warmed him.

After a pause, he said, "Leave them to it and come up and have a look at the view. It's above the mists."

"What about—"

"They'll be fine. For goodness' sake, they are basically adults now. Come on up and see the sun and view for a minute."

"Uh, Okay. I'll tell them and then come on up."

A few minutes later, there was a knock at the door from the elevator hub.

"Just come in, Sam," Kelvin said.

She went in through one of the doors. She didn't check the label. In the event, she entered the dining room. She strolled through to find Kelvin in the sitting area with drink in hand, sun shining on his face through the windows.

"Drink?" Kelvin said

"No. Just the view. The view will do just fine. You sure I can't tempt you away from your lovely apartment to watch the kids have fun?" Sam scanned the internal decor and smiled. "Some nice touches."

"Thank you. Mostly my doing. Myra wasn't too keen on '*input*.'"

"Why not?"

"She disapproved of some of the stuff I wanted on show."

Kelvin tipped his head in the direction of an ornate display cabinet filling one of the walls.

Sam walked over to the cabinet, open-mouthed. The cabinet was full of objects that were mostly seen only in books now. Science and technology had brought a creeping disaster to the world. Who knew what those two demons might bring in the future? Most of the fancy tech, like Artificial Intelligence, Drones and Multifunction Bulbs, was no longer permitted for ordinary folk. The rich and the criminally inclined seemed to be exempt from the rules, but it was ever thus.

"Aren't these things all illegal now?"

"I suppose so, but who will check on me in this city? I can pretty much do as I please."

Sam, still looking at the objects, said, "But you don't use them, do you?"

Kelvin turned away from the outlawed tech and changed the subject.

"Let me show you the view." Kelvin slipped an arm around Sam's waist, and she tensed slightly.

"Look. You can see the new buildings poking through the mist. Just like the old ones that poke through the waves in the bay."

Sam moved towards the window, but there was a definite emphasis on moving away from Kelvin, too. His arm stayed around her waist, and he instinctively followed her lead.

"It's a stunning view. You must be proud."

Kelvin could feel the rush of the alcohol. Disinhibition was washing over him.

"Come and see the bedroom."

Sam stiffened, and Kelvin did not. He suddenly realised that he sounded like a schoolboy.

After an interminable pause, he said, "No worries. The view can come around to us."

"No. Let's go and see the children. They are so keen to see you." Sam said, still with a stiffness in her voice.

"You go on down. I'll be down in a bit," Kelvin said.

Sam said nothing but was pleased to be heading back down to the children.

Kelvin wanted the sea mist to envelope him, but he also felt the sun on his back on the tenth floor.

He grabbed another drink. *"Come and see the bedroom. She knew what I wanted, and she made me feel small. I don't bloody well deserve that after all I've done for them."*

He downed his drink and poured yet another. He felt disinclined to join Sam and all the kids playing down below. Alone, and with his thoughts of what he had wanted to do with her, Kelvin decided to do some of his own playing down below, on the tenth floor.

9

Trade had been poor for the port city of Tangreco. Mid-sized ships, more correctly called large boats, were now the staple of the docks. It had been almost five years since the city had seen a large ship. This one was easily in that category, but it was not too big to navigate in the mouth and lower reaches of the river. However, it dropped its anchor out in the bay, beyond the inundated skyscrapers.

Black smoke emanated from its funnel, signalling the owners' ability to access fuel and their inability to service the engines properly. There were no markings along the slate grey hull or superstructure. No flag was to be seen flying.

Anyone with experience working in the docklands knew that the ship represented a rare opportunity to work and earn a crust. They flocked, hopefully, to the water's edge and the ramshackle compound operated by Cody Warne. He ran the docks. He was the docks. Nothing happened there without his say-so. But in truth, Cody was allowed to run the docks so long as he made enough money to pay for the privilege. He was a young man with slicked-back brown hair. His face was adorned with black tattoos. A skull and crossbones sat centrally on the forehead, with each bone resting on an eyebrow. Below the right eye was a black devil's trident, and below the left was a depiction of an empty syringe. His career had taken off via the supply of syringes and their contents, which also accounted for his catchphrase "Crack on." He was insistent on the formality of being called "Mr Warne."

The knock on the door of his office took Cody a little by surprise.

"What is it?" Warne said, feet up on his desk.

"Mr Warne. A big ship has just arrived in the bay. Should we send out some boats to it?"

"No, Mike. Let's have a closer look before we commit."

Mike, as if by magic, produced a pair of binoculars and handed them to Warne.

"This is why you are my right-hand man," smiled Warne.

Together, they went to the upper deck of the compound building and scanned the bay.

"What to make of it, eh, Mike?"

"Might be money in it for us."

"Might be money in it for them."

Warne dropped the binoculars from his eyes. "Why is the ship not coming into port?"

Both men stood in silence for a while.

"I don't like it, Mike. Get all the boys together. First, let's move all our really valuable stuff, the tech and most of the drugs, to our place on the south side of the city. Just in case. Then get everyone armed in case the ship's company is not that peaceable."

"Mr Warne?"

"Get on with it, Mike. We may not have a lot of time. Crack on."

Mike returned half an hour later. "All done, Mr Warne."

"Thanks. Now, let's get a boat out there and offer a

welcome. Three men should do it. Expendables. Join me on the roof when they are on their way."

"Okay, Mr Warne."

Mike disappeared to the outer office to make arrangements, and Warne returned to the roof.

When Mike reappeared, both men watched their inflatable head out to the mouth of the Tangreco River toward the ship. It was about halfway to its destination when Warne said, "They are launching!"

Mike looked through his optics. "I can see six inflatables being lowered. And the same may be happening on the side we can't see, Mr Warne."

"That's too big to be a welcoming party! Get our lot back here if you can. Now."

Mike returned to the office, radioed the boat, and then went back to his boss's side.

Warne, with the glasses to his eyes, said, "Ten to twelve chasing our boat in. All faster and bigger than ours. If they are hostiles, and I think they are, then we've lost those men and a boat. Let's get sorted on defending this place when they get here. Crack on, Mike."

Mike had turned pale and left without the usual formality of addressing his boss by name.

Cody stood on the flat rooftop of his compound buildings and watched the chase for a few minutes before descending to his office to make a call.

"We have a problem in the bay, Mr Kraxler,"

"Then sort it out, Warne."

The lack of politeness irritated Cody, but he knew better than to voice it.

"We may not have the resources. I think it's a raiding ship from along the coast. I have heard from contacts outside the city of such ships and raiders. They will not want to leave empty-handed. They may be spoiling for a fight, too, and it looks like we are outnumbered."

"I pay you to keep the docks and all that they contain safe. All they contain being mine!"

"Mr Kraxler—"

"Warne! Take it on the chin. Get our stuff, especially the good stuff, out of reach. Then we wait. We wait and see what we can negotiate."

"Mr Kraxler—"

"Crack on, Cody."

Kelvin cut the call and started a new one.

After a few moments, the connection was made.

"Floyd. I need your help." Kelvin said.

"Floyd Taylor, at your service as always. And, as always, it will cost you."

"And, as always, I pay you well and promptly because of your skillset and loyalty."

"And, as always, I will melt away, with none but my trusted knowing that I was anywhere near. That I was anywhere. That I was anyone."

"Maybe stop talking and get you and your team down to Teath docks. Pick me up on the way. I'm at home, not the office. I need to see this in person."

Floyd's team was contained within three black SUVs. The convoy rolled into the Kraxler driveway and stopped outside the front of the house. Floyd exited the first SUV, walked back to the middle one and opened its passenger door.

"I'll drive if you don't mind," Kelvin said.

Floyd looked at Kelvin and raised his right eyebrow. He could only raise one eyebrow. The other seeming slightly weak, adding to the overall effect of a somewhat droopy left side.

"You're the boss,"

Front seat shuffling occurred, and the convoy proceeded towards the docks with Floyd in the passenger seat next to Kelvin.

Kelvin called Cody while he drove.

"What's happening?"

"Twelve boats heading into the river. They have captured our exploratory boat and crew," Warne said.

"On our way."

Kelvin did not look like a happy man.

"Floyd, do you have people who can quietly immobilise twelve inflatables?"

"Why?"

"Do you?"

"The team in the rear vehicle can do it."

"Okay. Get more backup to replace them and get them down to the river. I want none of those inflatables to return to the ship in the bay."

Floyd made the arrangements, and the convoy split up.

Kelvin stopped the car and took out of his pocket a now-illegal piece of tech. On its screen, via a feed from the top of his building, he watched the boats come in and moor up along the quayside of Cody's compound.

"Inflatables have come ashore at Warne's compound. Get them all disabled," Kelvin said.

"My men are on their way to disable the boats."

Kelvin did not reply and resumed the drive to Warne's compound.

The inflatable armada had roughly the same number of men as those gathered in Warne's compound. Both factions were similarly equipped, but a boat could only hold a limited amount of ammunition.

Warne had spread most of his men around the compound, but he kept six of his best with him, discreetly armed.

"Okay. We are the welcoming party. Look busy around the place as if we are not expecting visitors."

Cody walked towards the harbour side of the compound to where the lead boat had alighted.

Politeness was all around. Warne said, "Throw me your line."

The leader did so, and the other boats tied up alongside.

"We have come to trade."

"Excellent. I am Mr Cody Warne."

"You don't need to know my name."

"What do you want to trade?"

The unidentified trader waved his arm at the boats, and his men dragged over six sobbing children.

"What?" Warne said.

"We will trade these Tangreco children for connectable tech or drugs."

"Mr Warne! I get confused, so please use my title when you address me," Cody intervened with exasperation.

No Name ignored this and spread his arms wide at the captive children, but said nothing.

Warne said nothing, and seconds passed.

"Okay, Mr Warne, here we have a standoff."

"It's only a standoff if we cannot agree terms. I cannot agree to your terms as I do not have what you want."

"You do. We have information about you from a reliable source."

"As we are both busy men, perhaps we should not waste time. My proposition is that you release all except one of the children of Tangreco, and in return, your men can search this compound for what you seek. They will not find anything, though, and when they find nothing, you will release the final child. Your source is not as reliable as you might think."

After a time, these terms were agreed upon, and children and men shuffled in the compound. One sobbing child was kept in front of No Name whilst the others were taken away to safety. The search of the compound started, leaving Cody facing No Name, with the small child interposed. A gun was pointing at the child, although she was unaware of it.

Kelvin halted the convoy just above and behind Warne's compound. Through the binoculars, he could see the activity on the waterfront.

"Floyd. None of these people must leave."

"Understood, Mr Kraxler." Floyd deployed his men, leaving one with Kraxler in the front SUV.

"What is your opinion of collateral damage, Mr Kraxler?"

"The same as you, I suspect, Floyd."

Floyd nodded his assent, snatched his weapon and headed into the compound. He made his way to the roof of a container with a view of the waterside negotiations. He lay prone, watching through the gun's scope. Through his scope, Floyd had a clear shot at No Name. He brought gentle pressure to bear on the trigger. Then he squeezed. As he squeezed, he slightly dipped the barrel of the weapon and fired two shots.

Gunfire erupted around the compound.

The child stopped crying.

No Name joined her, motionless on the floor.

Negotiations had ended. Floyd gave himself a crooked smile, got up and returned to Kraxler in the SUV.

"Seems you have a few spare inflatables now," Floyd said.

"I will sell them to help pay your bill. Now, please take me to my office."

10

The studio was located in a small complex in the southern part of the city. The first floor was his accommodation, and the second floor was his studio proper, overlooking the dockland area in the south of the city. Not much happened in the docks. Most of the action took place in larger commercial docks at the mouth of the river.

Carlos was covered in clay. That was his condition most days now.

He sat at his potter's wheel and threw for hours on end. It detached him from the world. He liked the silence of it.

His wheel was mechanically driven and creaked rhythmically as he pushed the treadle back and forth with his foot.

The creaking counted as silence. Actual silence was not silence for him. The noises of the Oakwood massacre constantly intruded on any silence. The gunshots. The screams of his parents. The silence of his dead father also counted as a sound. He liked the creaking. He liked having his own place, his own place to hide from memories.

Carlos slid the wire under the pot and slid it onto a drying bat. He carried it over to the large sill and looked out of the window. He could see the vessels moored in the southern docks. They were mostly pleasure craft that gave little pleasure any more as the cost and inability to acquire fuel made them effectively redundant. There were more and more sailing boats these days, with no need for fuel. Directly below the window, between the building and the water, was a now quiet road. Carlos spotted two people walking along the waterside towards his building. He smiled and turned back into his room to clean himself up.

A few moments later, the buzzer sounded and Carlos pressed the switch to open the door. He knew his visitors. He went over to the inner door, opened it and stood there waiting as the footsteps on the stairs got closer and closer.

"Do you two go everywhere together now?" Carlos asked, smiling.

Victor and Sienna just looked at each other, said nothing and shrugged.

"I see," Carlos said slowly. "Come on in. I'll get us all a drink. What are you two doing down here anyway?"

"Two beers if you have them," said Sienna.

"I do."

Victor carried on the conversation as if trying to thread large wooden blocks onto delicate fishing line. "This is a nice place, Carlos. Good for you to have your own place now. About time for that, really. Studio and somewhere to lay your head. Nice colours. Nice views."

Carlos raided his refrigerator and produced three cold beers.

"So..." Carlos said.

"So, yes," Victor said.

Carlos was lost for a few moments.

"It's nice to see you both, but I feel I am missing something here?"

"Carlos. It's not often I ask you for advice, is it?" Victor said.

"Uh, no." Carlos studied their faces.

"So we are brothers, right?" Victor said.

"Yep. Brothers and sisters," Sienna said.

"Well, only kind of." Carlos chipped in. "Well, yeah. Sienna is not actually our sister, but I think of her as our sister, and so does everyone else."

"And that's the problem," Sienna said.

"Why is it a problem?"

"Because I don't think of her as a sister," Victor said.

"And I don't think of him as a brother. But I do think of you as a brother, Carlos."

A second hand rotated very slowly in Carlos's head. "Oh…" A wave of understanding eventually washed over Carlos's face.

"So you two are… what… a thing?" Carlos continued.

"We are. But let's keep it a bit quiet, especially from Kelvin."

"Take the drinks downstairs. I'll be down in a few minutes," Carlos instructed.

A few minutes later, Carlos came down the steps, having changed his clothes and cleaned himself up. Victor and Sienna had opened the three beers and sat together on one of the two small sofas. Carlos deposited himself in the other one.

"What's up with you? You had a big smile for us upstairs. It's gone." Victor said to Carlos.

Carlos tried to bring the smile back, but with only partial success.

"Nice try, little brother, but what's up? You will always be my brother, even if I have a girlfriend or partner or whatever."

"I know that."

"Then why the long face?" Sienna asked.

"You will have a girlfriend too someday. Soon, I expect." Victor said.

"No, I won't."

"You will." Victor encouraged again.

"No, I won't because I don't want one!" Carlos explained.

"You will!" Victor promised.

Sienna looked at Victor. It was a special look. A look that took quite a bit of deciphering for a man.

"Sometimes, Victor, you are a bit slow to understand," Sienna said.

Victor turned to look at her and then back to his brother. Now the second hand rotated very slowly in Victor's head. "Oh. I see. I mean, I think I see."

Sienna decided to take control. "Yes, Victor, you do see and hopefully understand."

"I understand," Victor said, the mists of confusion slowly clearing. "And you will always, always, always be my brother. It is my job to look after you. It's been my job since the day we left Oakwood. It will always be my job."

Victor picked up his beer and concentrated greatly upon it, disinclined to further speech.

Silently, the three of them sat on the sofas, considering their newly divulged secrets.

11

"Samantha, how is everything?" Kelvin said into the phone.

"Fine, thank you, Kelvin." But she thought, *"He normally calls me Sam. Something is going on here."*

"How are you enjoying the new house? How are you enjoying being our neighbours?"

She couldn't lie. "The house is fantastic. It's not really new anymore, though, is it? We've been in it for five years, almost… The house is wonderful. The beach is beautiful. The neighbours could be better, I suppose."

She hoped that Kelvin thought that the last bit was a joke, even though it wasn't.

Kelvin took it as a joke and continued. "Well, I think it could be better. I think we missed a couple of things when we designed it. It could do with a bit more security. Yours and ours."

"Really?"

"Better safe than sorry these days."

"Have you chatted to Elliott about it?"

"Elliott is great with the business thing. Homes are the province of the fairer sex, so I am coming to you first."

"Uh, Okay. What do you want to do?"

"You free at the moment?"

"Not really. I was just about to pay Carlos a visit. Why?"

"Well, then, that's good. I am at the office. You have to pass me to get to Carlos's place. Drop by on your way and take a quick look at the plans. It will take ten minutes, that's all. Then I will show them to Elliott later when he returns to the office."

"Uh… Where's Myra? Has she looked at them?"

"She's not interested, to be honest. She's gone to visit Isabella, I think."

Sam thought, *When people say 'To be honest,' it usually means it's a lie.*

"Why don't we all look at your plans together later when we are all around?"

An edge arrived in Kelvin's voice. "So you and your family are living in a beautiful house that I have paid for, and yet you cannot spare me a few minutes to look at what I am proposing."

"Kelvin, that's not fair, and you know it!"

Kelvin did not reply and let the silence just hang there.

"Oh, okay. But just ten minutes." Sam eventually, and hesitatingly, replied.

Kelvin did not show her the same courtesy and just cut the call.

Sam kept the phone in her hand, which was now shaking slightly. *That man is getting worse. I wish we had never accepted his offer to take this new house next door to him.* She punched in Elliott's number, but the line refused to connect. Next, she called Carlos and told him she would be late.

12

Kelvin put the phone down and went over to the drinks cabinet. He made up his favourite drink and added ice.

He got the chilled wine from the cooler, opened it and set it down next to the waiting wine glass.

"Twenty minutes, I think. Yeah, about that."

Kelvin drank his drink and poured another. He paced the room and then went to the bathroom. Expectation and drink set his pulse on fire. It had been a long time since his previous failed attempt to get Sam alone, and it added to his feelings.

Kelvin's hand shakily held the glass as he went through to the bedroom and placed papers on the table next to the window that looked out over the city.

It was another day, just like the last time he had tried to get her alone, of cold, rolling mists at street level and the sun above at the level of the apartment.

Kelvin forced himself to sit, and forced himself to not drink his drink.

At last, he settled. He sat, and he waited.

The Kraxlers and the Keoghs were well known to security at the Kraxler building. As Sam entered, the security detail nodded a quick hello as she headed for the elevator to the penthouse apartment and offices on the top floor.

"I'll be back down in a few minutes. Just a flying visit," she said to the security man, who nodded again without speaking.

She punched in the code and waited for the doors to open. When they did, she tentatively stepped in. They closed behind her, and she rode up to the top floor.

Kelvin heard the elevator, quickly had another nervous gulp of his drink and headed for the elevator door. He got there just before it arrived and stood, drink in hand, as the doors opened.

"Sam. Come in. Come in. Thanks for coming by."

"No problem, Kelvin. I'm just off to see Carlos, as I said, so it will have to be quick."

"Maybe not too quick."

Kelvin gazed at Sam for a moment longer than was polite and then said, "Do you know your hair is almost the same colour as Sienna's? It's not quite as red, but it's almost there. He reached out to touch her hair, but she tilted herself away.

Kelvin paused, smiled, and guided her in, holding a drink in his left hand and aiming his right arm at Sam's waist.

She evaded it. "What do you want to show me, Kelvin?"

"It's in here. I've got your favourite wine open for you, too."

"Kelvin, I don't want a drink. I'm on my way to see Carlos."

"Carlos can wait," Kelvin said in a firm tone.

She looked at him. His face was all smiles, but his eyes gave a different message.

"I have to go. I can see your stuff another day." She turned to leave.

"You will see what I want you to see now!" Kelvin grabbed her wrist.

She tried to pull away, but he gripped it hard.

"Kelvin! Let go of me!"

"Come and have that drink." Kelvin dragged her towards the bedroom.

"LET GO OF ME!" She shouted.

"Gratitude! That's gratitude! All I've done for you and your so-called family! Come here!"

Kelvin yanked her by the arm. He yanked her so hard that she lost her footing. Sam had gone silent.

"Get up!" Kelvin lifted her by her arm as she struggled to regain her balance.

She just about managed to regain her footing as he continued to drag her towards the bed. Continuing the motion, she swung her legs under his, whilst trying to drop to the floor, pulling them both to the floor. She kicked out in the hope of connecting with any tender part of his body, but he backed away enough that she didn't connect. He rolled on top of her, pinning her down. She could smell the drink on his breath as he pressed his lips to hers. He pulled back and smiled. Then dropped his face forward for another kiss.

As their lips met, Kelvin felt her mouth open in welcome. Joy flooded through him at the apparent conquest. Her mouth opened wider, and then she lunged up at him, sinking her teeth into his lower lip. She could taste the blood, and she could hear him scream, but she did not let go. He tried to pull his face away, but the pain was too much. He rolled his body away from on top of her, but still, she did not slacken her bite. She wriggled and managed to get above him. The pain in his lip was so bad that he just had to follow whichever way she guided him. She managed to get to her knees, kneeling over his face.

She released him and leapt to her feet. She ran for the door. Kelvin moved faster than he had in years and darted after her, blood running down his chin. He didn't care about subtle conquests or anything else now. He was crazed. Sam reached the door and managed to open it. He dived and he caught her ankle, flooring her once again. Her arms crashed to the floor in front of her, dislodging her wristwatch and sending it towards the open door. She rolled onto her back, and he clambered over her.

"Bitch! Bitch! Bitch!" He spat at her, covering her face with a spattering of bloody drool. She lifted her head and spat right back at him.

He pulled her back into the room. Kelvin grabbed her head by the ears and smashed the back of her head against the marble floor. She stopped spitting. He let go, and her head hit the floor again with a dull thud. There was also a much quieter sound, which Kelvin Kraxler did not hear. A tiny tinkling sound.

Blood flowed from her left earlobe.

"It was supposed to be the bed, but you deserve it on the floor." Kelvin thought.

He quietly hissed at her prone form, "Bitch!"

He undid her trousers and pulled them down. Grinning, he did the same with his own.

Looking down, he noticed that despite his earlier excitement, he now needed a little self-encouragement to achieve a successful outcome.

There were other things that he did not immediately notice.

13

Sienna and Connie sat together at lunch. They were in an upmarket bar-come-restaurant on the waterfront in the Erth district of the city. They were monied. They could afford it. The view was impressive. Out to sea, they could see the inundated skyscrapers of the old city. The scene was calm, with virtually no shipping going in or out of the docks. Aromas from the kitchen had set the digestive juices flowing. While they waited in hungry anticipation of lunch, the two sisters chatted away.

"What will you do with yourself if you move out of the city?" Sienna asked Connie.

"Farm."

"What, just farm?"

"I have already started. I really don't like the city any more. I mean, this is great, but to sit in a nice place and do nice things whilst there are so many others in the city that are struggling to get by... It doesn't feel right. Look at this place. It is stunning, but they have to have security guards, and we have to be careful getting to and from the place."

"You got a farm! Where is it?"

"It's in the mountains to the south of the city. Isabella found it for me."

"Found it?"

"Yep. She has hidden depths, don't you think?"

"I think you may be right."

"What sort of farm is it? Don't you have to be there?"

"I have been there. That's why I haven't been around much. There are a couple of people who live out that way. Nearby. They look after the place when I'm not around. I do the same for them. They were there before I got it. I don't disturb them. They look after, and use, the farmhouse when I'm away."

"I wish you wouldn't go."

"Well, you are with Victor almost all of the time now."

"Only when he's not working for Dad."

"You are a couple. You won't want me hanging around. Besides, you know me. Bit of a loner and nature lover."

"True. Also, a bit weird. And you love all that outlawed tech from before The Yielding."

"Uh, true also. But I use it responsibly. I can interact with people without having to interact with them. I can get information when I want it, when the kit works."

"You can get locked up too!"

"Come on! That's pretty unlikely. Dad runs most things in the city." Connie said.

"Mmm," Sienna said. It wasn't clear if she was disagreeing with her sister's position of admiring the arrival of their food.

"Speaking of which, why don't we drop in and see him? He goes on enough about the view from the top floor. And it's only a couple of minutes' walk away."

"Well, I suppose it might keep him quiet about it for a while."

They parked the chat and tucked into the food.

Sienna nodded at the waiter and indicated that they were finished and were leaving. They paid the bill and headed for the door.

"Do you need someone to escort you?" said the door guard.

"No, thank you," Sienna said. 'We will be fine, thank you."

They left the bar and headed down the street, turning left to approach the Kraxler building.

"Should we let him know we are coming?" Connie said.

"No need. He will be there and will be eager to show off the view."

"Mother might be there too."

"I doubt it. She prefers the house, away from the business and away from the eyes of most of the city."

As they approached the Kraxler building, Connie said, "So, you and Victor are good together, right?"

"It's like we know each other so well after all this time, but it also feels new. I suppose it's a bit weird, but I don't expect anyone other than Dad to be that bothered by what his favourite daughter gets up to."

Connie smiled. "He doesn't know what I get up to!"

They both smiled, went into the building, and headed for the elevator.

The security man nodded at them both, and they smiled back. He watched them as the elevator doors closed behind them.

"Do you know what goes on the other floors?" Connie said.

"No idea." Connie randomly jabbed at the panel and pressed the button for the eighth floor. "Let's see, shall we?" A mischievous sparkle in her eye.

The elevator doors opened onto a landing. In front of them was a large door, and a keypad to the right of it.

"Do you know the code?" Sienna asked Connie.

"No, but we may not need one. Look."

Connie pointed at the keypad. Just above it was a small

built-in camera.

"Fancy pants Dad likes his gizmos. Our biometrics can get us into the building. Maybe they can get us into this room."

Connie moved in front of the camera and pressed a button on the keypad. The door opened.

"Yes! Come on, let's take a look around." Connie said.

They both entered the eighth-floor storage room.

They knew that their father traded objects and things that were technically illegal, but this entire floor was stacked with illegal tech and guns. The shelves and storage containers were floor-to-ceiling, and the room was full, except for the access lanes between them.

"He better not find out that we have been in here," Sienna said.

"I know. He would burst a blood vessel."

"Look at all this stuff."

"Come on, Sienna. Let's get out of here and go up to ten and see the old man."

"Okay. Better we don't know about this sort of thing anyway."

14

Kelvin found himself on all fours with his trousers around his knees. Bloody drool dripped from his lower lip. The self-encouragement hadn't worked, and the outcome was definitely unsuccessful.

"Bitch." But more quietly from Kelvin. "Wake up."

He looked down at Sam.

She's not breathing.

He moved forward and shook her, trousers almost comically around his knees. He shook her, but he got no response.

"Shit! Shit! Shit! What have I done!" Kelvin whispered to the room.

He stood up, only half gathering his trousers, snatched the internal phone and punched the security button.

The pick-up was prompt. "Yes, Mr Kraxler?"

"Let no one else up here until I give you the say-so."

"Are you okay, Mr Kraxler? Your voice sounds strange."

"Fine. Do as I say. No one else up here until I tell you."

"Mr Kraxler—"

Kelvin cut the call.

The security man stopped telling the dead phone that the Kraxler girls were on their way up.

* * *

Kelvin shuffled over to the desk, gravity-stricken trousers impeding his progress. He grabbed the phone and punched in a number.

After several seconds, he said, "Floyd. I need you here at the new Kraxler building now."

"It will take me only minutes."

"With a team of two others who can be trusted."

Kelvin took a breath and thought. *"All under control,"*

He hoisted his trousers and closed them. Then he put a hand to his lower lip to feel the damage. He looked towards the lifeless body of Samantha Keogh. His eyes caught sight of her watch on the floor in the open doorway. They also caught sight of a pair of female legs standing in the doorway. He raised his eyes and stared into those of his elder daughter.

15

Kelvin was rooted to the spot.

Sienna was not. She slammed the door shut, turned, grabbed Connie, and headed for the elevator.

She was pale and had an unreadable expression. "Go. Go to your farm and don't come back until I tell you it's okay. Please!"

Sienna called the elevator. The doors opened straight away. Sienna pushed Connie in.

"Go! I will call you. Don't come back until I tell you it's okay." Sienna whispered.

The elevator doors closed.

The door to the apartment opened, and Kelvin stepped out.

Silently, father and daughter faced each other.

"Was anyone with you?" Kelvin asked in a strangely quiet voice.

Sienna's face, framed by her red hair, glared at him. Her green eyes the only colour in her face.

"You..." she managed.

Kelvin, almost inaudible, said, "Yes, with you. Was there anyone with you?"

His eyes lifted to the elevator floor indicator. It was

heading to the ground floor.

Sienna tried to speak. "Da..." But she couldn't finish the word.

"Sienna," he whispered. You don't understand. It's not—"

"It is exactly what it is."

"Sienna. It's not what you think."

Kelvin's eyes welled up, and small tears escaped them. Sienna had never seen her father cry. He lifted his hands and rubbed away the tears. When his hands fell away, his expression was different.

"Was anyone with you? I can find out easily enough, you know." His voice was also different—stronger, more robust and more defiant.

Sienna looked straight at her father and asked in a quivering voice. "Why?"

"Why? Why do we do anything, Sienna? Because we want to. Everything we do is because we want to. We want to love our children. We want to love and protect our families. We want to have the ability to fulfil our wants and our needs. Sometimes, our wants do not coincide with the wants of others."

It was the turn of Sienna's eyes to leak now. "How do I not know you?"

As Kelvin opened his mouth to speak, the elevator door opened behind Sienna.

Sienna turned, expecting to see Connie. She didn't see Connie. She saw three men. The first one out of the elevator, the obvious leader, had a droopy left eyelid.

He looked straight at Kelvin. He didn't even seem to notice that Sienna stood there. "What can I do for you, Mr Kraxler?"

"Sienna here is my daughter. She has had a bit of a shock. I would like you to take her away and look after her. Take her somewhere safe and comfortable. Make sure that she has everything she needs. She has had a big shock and is upset.

We don't want to worry anyone else, so we need to keep this confidential in the extreme. This is very important to me, Floyd."

"We can do these things," Floyd said.

"I know. Are these two men with you reliable enough for the task?"

Floyd turned to them, and they both silently nodded."

"Confidential in the extreme, Floyd. Do your men understand what that means?"

"They do. Everything my men do is confidential."

"Okay. Get on with it. You stay here, Floyd."

Kelvin turned away and returned to the apartment. "Close the door on your way in, Floyd," he said.

Kelvin checked with security, "Has anyone just come down in the elevator?"

"No one, Mr Kraxler," came the reply.

Sienna had been looking around her whilst the men had been talking. She couldn't enter her father's apartment, and three men were between her and the elevator. There was a door to the stairwell, which she might get to, but she doubted it.

Floyd stepped forward to follow Kelvin. He had to step around Sienna, who still hadn't moved.

Floyd turned to his men and nodded. "What are you waiting for?" he said to his men. "Take her anywhere safe for now. Treat her well. Arrangements will be made."

Floyd followed Kelvin in and closed the door. Outside it, the two men took Sienna by the arms and guided her to the elevator. She did not resist them at all. One of the men pressed the button for the ground floor.

Sienna let her legs collapse beneath her and started what appeared to be a full-body convulsion, but she did not attempt to break the men's grip. The men looked at each other, concern written on their faces, and tried to turn Sienna around to lay her on the elevator floor. Both men, as a result, loosened their grip on her wrists. Sienna's feet were just outside the elevator doors, which began to close.

Connie had fallen back into the elevator car. She scrambled to her feet. The look on her sister's face had chilled her to the bone. She had never seen Sienna look like that in all of her life. She pressed the button to descend to the ground floor and then, without thinking, immediately pushed the button for the eighth floor.

Thoughts raced through her mind. *What's happened here? Should I go back for Sienna? It must be something bad… should I run and get the hell out of here? What should I do?*

The elevator door opened, and Connie staggered onto the eighth-floor landing.

What should I do?

She was rooted to the spot. The sound of the elevator door beginning to close snapped her out of it. She exited the elevator, put her face in front of the entry camera, and pressed the button, exactly as Sienna had done earlier. The door opened, and she entered the room containing row upon row of illegal tech. She closed the un-windowed door behind her.

Thoughts about what she should do still swirled in her head, but she was drawn to the stuff on the shelves. She slowly wandered along the racks of kit, picking them up and replacing them as she went. Multifunction Bulbs, Global Communicators, AI Trackers. There were obvious weapons, too. From small, easily concealed projectile weapons to "Don't mess with me!" huge things that Connie doubted she would even be able to lift.

Take some of this stuff, she thought.

She did. Stuffing the pockets of her jacket with what she could easily carry.

She left the room in a daze and headed down the stairwell, avoiding the elevator. She then quietly left the building. Security remained unaware of her departure.

16

Sienna wrenched her hands away from her captors. She scrambled and wriggled, arms flailing, as the elevator doors continued to close. The two men were paralysed by indecision. They knew they must not hurt Sienna, but they had to keep her with them until Floyd made more permanent arrangements.

Sienna suddenly jerked upright and managed to get out of the elevator and to her feet. She ran for the stairwell door.

The elevator doors were as indecisive as her would-be captors. First, they shut upon the men, trapping their hands, and then opened again. When they finally decided to open fully, there was no sign of Sienna, but the door opposite the elevator showed a hint of movement.

The men looked at one another and gave chase.

"Wait. We need to take the elevator out of the equation. I'll follow her down the stairwell. You take the elevator down to ground level and either disable it or get that useless security man to keep it there. Then you come up the stairs. We will catch her between us."

"So you get to go down ten flights, and I get to go up ten!"

"Just do it!"

One headed back to the elevator. The other headed down

the stairwell. He couldn't hear her or see Sienna.

Sienna ran down two flights, paused, and listened. There were no sounds of anyone following her. Then she realised that this was the floor that she and Connie had visited only a few minutes before. She opened the door, went inside, and quietly closed the door. She pressed the lock button on the inside, and there was a small click.

Sienna ran the full length of the room to the window on the far side. The view from this window was almost identical to that from the penthouse.

She found no other way out. Quietly, she examined the shelves, waiting to be found, as she dared not return to the stairwell.

She ran her hands along the shelves. She picked up a bag containing grey ovoid shapes that would comfortably fit into the palm of a hand. The bag was usefully labelled "KKMFB."

She'd heard of multifunction bulbs, but they were illegal now. The "KK" was an easy guess. She tore open the plastic bag and grabbed three MFBs.

Several minutes passed before a quiet click broke the silence. Sienna guessed that it must be the door. She knew that her only chance was to get out through the door through which she had entered. She moved stealthily to the far right of the windowed end of the room. She waited a few more seconds and then threw one of the MFBs to the far left corner. Then she crept around the right wall as quietly as she could, circling back to the door.

Hope rose as she saw no one at the door. She headed for it with growing hope as she heard footsteps to the left, where she had flung the MFB.

She opened the door and ran straight into the man with a droopy eye.

"If you want a job doing..." he said.

17

Floyd multitasked as he drove the car and received instructions over his phone. Sienna sat obediently in the passenger seat. The day's events had become surreal and utterly exhausting. Floyd's men sat in the rear. One had a gun on display.

"Okay. Have it ready in one hour and be out of the place. Two guards will be needed." Floyd slowed his driving and cut the call.

"Where are you taking me?" Sienna asked.

"Somewhere safe. Nice views."

"Where are you taking me?"

"Everything will be ready for your arrival in about an hour. Sit back and take a breath."

"Where—"

"Never mind. Stop asking me. You will be there in an hour."

Sienna decided to stop speaking. She closed her eyes and tried multitasking herself. She wanted to recall the recent events with her father, and she wanted not to recall the recent events with her father.

Floyd pulled the car into a side street and stopped. The four occupants sat in silence for about thirty minutes.

Then, Floyd started the motor.

"Blindfold her now. We don't want her to know exactly where she is going."

The man in the back seat, not toting a gun, obeyed.

"It won't be for long, Sienna. You will be fine." Floyd reassured.

Sienna was past fighting and meekly sat still, quiet and blind as Floyd drove through the city streets.

It wasn't long before the car stopped. Sienna heard Floyd get out, and the men behind her followed suit. Their doors slammed shut, and her door opened. Gently but firmly, hands guided her out of the car and into the warm air of a building. Floyd removed her blindfold and looked her in the eye. No words were exchanged, but the look he gave her had a clear meaning: *Behave!* She did.

The elevator took them up to the top floor, and they exited onto a landing. Two uniformed men stood outside a plain door. They perked up when they saw Floyd. One of the men opened the door.

Floyd turned to Sienna and said, "These men, or others like them, will always be outside your door and will look after you. They will get you whatever you want, within reason."

"My door?" Sienna questioned.

"Go in and make yourself at home. It will be your home for a while." Floyd replied.

Sienna went in, and the door closed behind her. The view of the city below was magnificent. It would be the only way she would experience the city for quite some time.

18

Kelvin was not a fan of the city police, but on this occasion, it seemed like their services would be more appropriate than those of his preferred, private operatives.

He put in a call to Tony. The same Tony that somehow had amassed much more wealth than his police salary would account for.

"Tony, I have a problem you can help me with."

"Anything to help," Tony said. There was just a hint of fear in his voice.

"I'm not sure that this has got to the police department yet. I have been dealing with it privately, for obvious reasons." Kelvin let the unknown hang in the air.

"What have you been dealing with?" Tony had to ask.

"My daughter, Sienna, is missing."

"We will do everything we can to find her. I will get my best team onto it straight away."

Kelvin paused for Tony's benefit.

"What else do you need, Mr Kraxler?"

Kelvin used silence again to unsettle Tony. Then he ploughed on.

"I... I think she has been abducted. Or worse. The difficulty is that I think... Well, I know who is responsible. He is someone quite close to my family." Kelvin paused again.

"How do you know? Who is it?"

"I know who it is, but I don't have any proof."

Again, Kelvin paused. Each pause was like a left hook to Tony's chin.

Kelvin decided to land the final blow.

"I'm sure the police will be able to find the evidence." Kelvin paused again.

Tony hesitated and then said, "I'm sure they will."

"Excellent." Kelvin used the pause again, but Tony had gathered himself a little now—each man duelling with the silence.

Kelvin became bored with the game. "Victor Atkar. He will be at his house tonight, I'm sure. I think it would be wise to make it his last night there. I also think that the cells in Vantuba Prison are pretty comfortable.

Kelvin ended the call.

19

It was another day in court for Kelvin, the verdict having been decided upon at an earlier hearing. Today, he decided that it would look better if he did not occupy the middle seat. He was seated with two others, both men, at the bench at the front of the court.

Directly in front of the bench was the dock, occupied by an empty chair. To the rear of the dock was a small public gallery. It contained Myra Kraxler, Leon Kraxler, Isabella Lightfoot, Elliott Keogh and Carlos Atkar.

Victor was brought into the courtroom through a side entrance, flanked by two armed guards, and placed in the dock. The judge in the centre of the Bench addressed Victor. "Please sit."

"I would rather stand," Victor announced.

"Well, we would prefer you to sit," the judge said.

Victor felt downward pressure on his shoulder from one of the guards.

He sat.

The three at the Bench murmured to each other, and all but Kelvin looked towards Victor.

"Compelling evidence of your involvement in the disappearance of Sienna Kraxler and Samantha Keogh has been presented to this court," the central judge opined. "Strongly compelling evidence, in fact. Evidence that you abducted the young woman or worse. Strong evidence, too, that you have also abducted, or worse, Samantha Keogh. She had shown you and your brother great kindness, taking you in off the streets. Less compelling evidence of their deaths has been presented to the court, so it may be that both women are still alive. Now is your opportunity to save them and yourself by confessing your misdeeds and telling us where they are so that they can be rescued."

There was once again silence in the room.

"Well?" the central judge said to Victor.

Victor stood up, turned to those behind him, and then turned back to face the bench. When he started to speak, the room knew that Victor was primarily addressing the families. The bench was, without a doubt, a secondary consideration for him.

"I would like to make it clear to everyone here that I know nothing about any of these things. Samantha and Elliott Keogh showed my brother and I exceptional kindness. Having lost our parents, they become our new parents. Neither of us would wish any harm to them. Sienna and Connie were like extra siblings for us, and we would wish them no harm either. I did not get on well with Leon Kraxler, or he with me, but I think that is because of a rivalry for Kelvin's affections and attentions. Whatever evidence you have before you is flawed. Or it is fabricated. I hope that both women are found safe and well."

Silence fell again, followed by whispers between the members of the bench.

"Your last chance, Atkar," the judge said.

Silence.

Eventually, the central judge cleared his throat and continued.

"Victor Atkar. You are guilty of the abduction of Samantha Keogh and Sienna Kraxler—the penalty for these crimes is life imprisonment. You will now be returned to Vantuba prison."

Victor turned away from the bench and spoke directly to the families at the back of the courtroom. "Thank you for all that you have done for me and Carlos. Thank you for all your kindness. I hope it all works out."

Victor turned back to the bench and said, "Mr Kraxler, I love both your daughters. I hope that one day Sienna will be found safe and well and… And that she and I can be together."

For the first time, Kelvin looked up at Victor. He said nothing. He lifted his right arm and pointed at the side entrance.

Part 2

20

One of the regular summer storms was approaching, becoming increasingly audible over the usual lockdown babble as the Vantuba prison shifted to nocturnal mode. The prison's design was a marvel of genius and idiocy, in equal measure. It meant that very few guards were needed to watch over the inmates.

Despite his youth and relative inexperience, Luc Moyes was old school. He could do all that was required of him from the comfort of his office, but he liked to walk one lap of the circular prison before lights out. Most inmates ignored his perambulations, but a few, like Victor, would chat with him.

"You good, Vic?"

"Buzzing, just buzzing, Mr Moyes."

"Must be the electricity of the storm. If the partying gets too rowdy—"

"I'll keep it down as always."

Victor sat on his bunk at the back of his cell, eyes closed, listening and tracking the routine of the prison lockdown in his head. Another twenty minutes and the general lighting would change to partial illumination, and then the cells themselves would be claimed by darkness.

Victor memorised the timings of these things as well as the internal layout of the place. Just to keep his mind active. When allowed out of his cell, he would try to make his way around with his steely blue eyes closed. He had been in the place long enough to have almost mastered it.

"Another storm on the way, Vic, your favourite."

"We are safe enough in here. From the storm, at least." Victor pushed himself further back on his bunk at the back of his cell. "Night, Mr Moyes."

"Sleep like a baby, Vic, sleep like a baby."

Victor replied with silence and tucked his knees up under his chin. Lightning had once struck his house as a boy, and he had been terrified of it ever since.

What dimwit put a prison on top of a cliff? He thought.

He wasn't sure if it was himself or the cell walls shaking. Then, a huge crash and a rumble through the entire building ended any doubts. Instantly, all the lights went out, plunging the whole place into complete darkness.

The electronic lock on his cell door clicked open, and he leapt from his bunk. The bars to his cage opened with ease. Shouting from the other inmates told him that the same release from close incarceration had happened to them, too. Victor listened as the entirety of the prison's population flooded onto the landings and stairwells.

Where are you now, Mr Moyes? He thought.

Victor waited just outside his cell, listening as the chaos mounted. His eyes became more used to the darkness, but he could still see very little. He could hear the main throng moving to the main stairwell and then down to the ground-floor exercise area and the main entrance to the prison. All were looking for guards to attack and hardware to destroy or damage. Still, he waited. He knew the power might be restored at any moment. He decided to go in the opposite direction to the mob, upwards to the fourth floor and the control centre. He passed no one on the way to the stairwell. As he climbed, he became aware that a dim red light was helping his vision and that he could smell smoke. The idiots in the central atrium had stripped anything movable and started an indoor bonfire without working out how they themselves would escape the flames. They would soon realise their plight and return to the upper floors, bringing the chaos with them.

Victor climbed the stairs and reached the control room door.

"Mr Moyes, you in there?"

Silence.

"Moyes, you in there? The party has definitely gotten a bit rowdy. We both need to get out of here. Come on - we have to go. You won't leave this place alive once that lot gets up here. Come on, for fuck sake!"

The door opened. Moyes came out, turned, and locked it from the outside. He said nothing and headed down the still-dark corridor. Victor followed. Smoke and heat were rising around them. Ahead, a service elevator and stairwell were just about visible in the gloom.

The blow caught Luc in the gut, and he crumpled to the floor, gasping for air. Victor arrived a second later. The wooden baton was raised above the shoulders of a dark shadow, directly over Luc's prone figure. Victor lunged at its midriff, instinct driving him forward. Given the usual "us and them" of prison life, it was a strange, unintelligible instinct. Victor carried on his charge, smashing the other inmate into the service elevator door. His right shoulder pushed forward and upwards into his solar plexus, gaining him a fraction of a second. He pulled back slightly to give himself room and swung his left fist upwards, catching the figure between the lower jaw and hyoid bone, sending the man's head crashing against the elevator doors. The inmate slumped to the floor with a dreadful wheezing as his unconscious brain attempted to get oxygen past the spasm of vocal cords barring its entry.

Victor turned to Moyes. "You okay?"

"Will be."

"We need to go, or we are both dead meat."

"Get me up. I have the keys to the stairwell."

"I could just take them and run."

Still struggling to stand up straight and get air in and out, Moyes said quietly, "Yes… Yes, you could."

"Give me the key."

Moyes reached for the ring and staggered forward toward the door. Hands shaking, he inserted the key and turned the lock. With one motion, Victor pushed Moyes aside, grasped the keys, and went through the door, leaving Moyes crouched, hands on knees over the wheezing inmate. The door closed and locked behind Victor, leaving Moyes to the rising inmates and the smoke.

Then the key turned again, and the door reopened.

Victor grabbed Moyes by the collar and dragged him through the door, closing and locking it behind them.

"Down, I presume?"

"Down, but not down and out."

"The last word of that sentence is pretty important for me."

"Can't help you *out,* Vic."

"No."

They continued down the stairwell to the prison's ground floor, neither man in familiar surroundings.

"Three doors."

"All of them locked."

"Please open them, Mr Moyes."

"Can't do it, Vic."

"If you force the issue, I will take your keys."

"No, I mean, I can't open them all. I only have a key to take us through that one."

"Which leads to?"

"Kitchens."

"Let's go cook then."

"You still won't get out, though."

"Let's open it up and see. We are trapped if the crowd manages to get through any of the upper doors. It's probably not a problem for me, but a big one for you. Let's go cook."

Moyes studied his keys in the gloom. On his third attempt, he found the one that opened the door to the kitchens, and they went through.

Suddenly, the lights came back on, and the thunderclaps had to compete with deafening alarms.

"How do we get out of the kitchen?"

"I can't help you *out,* Vic."

"Just out of the kitchens."

After some thought, Luc said, "Three ways out. The way we came in, through the far door into the burning dining hall and its party, or down the garbage chute."

"So, technically, the garbage chute leads out of the kitchens and out of the prison?"

"Doesn't help you though."

"Where does the garbage go?"

"Down."

"Down?"

"Down to the river."

"Oh!"

"It seems that we both have two choices: sit and wait here or take the rapid, uncontrolled descent to the river."

"I'm not sure which option I prefer, but I want the option. I need to find the opening to the chute."

"I can't help you *out,* Vic."

"I know, but if that lot out there becomes that lot in here, I might be helping *you* out."

"There it is, in between those units."

Victor removed a circular cover and inserted his head into the now exposed tubular opening. The rank odour soon made him remove it again.

"It's wide enough, but I can't see the other end. There must be a flap or something because I can't hear the storm either. You got a torch, Mr Moyes?

"In the office."

Victor cast his eyes over the kitchen. He found some paper towels and cooking oil. He soaked the paper in the oil, lit it on the gas stove and threw it into the chute."Just a load of rotting waste food at the bottom. Getting back up would be nearly impossible. Too steep a slope and too slippery."

Victor returned his attention to the kitchen's contents, looking for inspiration. A stack of clean towels on a steel cage caught his eye.

"You any good with knots, Mr Moyes?"

"I can't help you *out,* Vic."

The noise from the main dining area was lessening, as the fire drove the inmates back to the upper levels. As yet, there was no noise from the stairwell down which they had descended, either.

"If that lot gets in here, you won't have any choice but to help yourself out. Your gun will only take out a few of the mob. The rest will get you."

Luc was starting to seem like a rabbit caught in the dazzle of headlights.

"Help me with this." Victor dragged the cage and towels to the chute entrance, looped a towel through the cage, and tied another towel to the first, then another and another.

"Do I have to spell this out for you, Mr Moyes?"

No reply.

"Okay then. Towel rope is thrown down the chute. I go down the chute without you helping me *out*. If I decide to climb back up, then no harm done. If you need a place to hide from the mob on your heels, you have a hiding place behind the towels and cage. You can return for a decent shower and a change of clothes by climbing back up the towel rope once your teammates restore order."

Luc looked dubious and stood watching Victor make the towel rope. He then went to the foot of the stairwell to listen for any intrusion.

"Which will it be through the door first, Mr Moyes… Guards or prisoners?"

Pounding and then a crash from above told them they wouldn't have long to find out. Without speaking, Luc headed for the chute. Victor was already dropping feet-first over the lip. Luc got there too late to follow. The towel crate had already obstructed the opening. Try as he might, he couldn't pull it back with all of Victor's weight on it. The prisoner mob was getting closer to the foot of the stairwell, voices raised, full of anger. Luc pushed on one side of the crate and rotated it just enough to get his body between it and the chute, but his back was towards the wall. He leaned backwards into the chute, gripping the towel as he went, and the towel crate crashed back against the wall, hiding the entrance from view.

The mob entered the kitchen, led by the inmate Victor had taken out at the top of the stairs. Luc could see them through the crate in the kitchen lights, but he remained unnoticed in the darkness of the chute.

"Dignified exit, Mr Moyes," whispered Victor.

Luc's head was now only inches above Victor's. "I'm not going out headfirst."

"Well, you aren't going to turn around in here in a hurry, are you—"

Suddenly, the towel rope gave way from above, and both men slid further down the chute, both holding the now flaccid towel. Victor's feet hit the detritus pile at the bottom of the chute. He slowed but didn't stop as the outer cover of the chute tilted open. Luc was a fraction of a second behind him, and with an undignified head butt into the rotting food, he completed the task of opening the chute to the storm outside. Victor slid on, still holding the towels, Luc just behind. Luc managed to hitch the towels over the upper part of the circular cover as he, too, exited the chute. Both men dangled there, not daring to speak or move. Below them was a pile of rotting food and waste on a slightly sloping platform cut into the cliff face. Above them was a ten-meter vertical rock face, and the verticality continued for an unknown distance below the platform. Rain soaked them, and the strong wind chilled them, despite the season..

"Up or down, Mr Moyes?"

"Down onto the platform first of all. I can't hold this towel for much longer."

"Let go then. We are only about a meter above the platf—"

Luc let go and dropped into the spoil pile. Victor kept hold but dropped too, and the towel rope eventually jammed on the hinge mechanism above. It was slippery as hell. Victor steadied himself with the aid of the jammed rope. Luc gripped Victor around the midriff. Both men used their feet to push themselves back against the wall and away from the edge, sending the food pile over the edge. Scavenger birds screeched their displeasure. Both men sat back against the wall and took a breath.

"Can you hear that?" Victor said, pointing up at the chute.

"Just, I think."

They looked up at the chute's cap, which was still half open and entangled with the towels.

From the chute came a cry, followed by a dull thud and a

rusty squeak.

A prison guard dropped limply past their heads onto the slippery sloping platform and slid to the edge. Luc's arm reached out, but the bloodied body went over the edge.

Victor counted.

21

Kelvin sat in *his* armchair in *his* penthouse apartment on the top floor of *his* building, waiting for *his* wife to arrive. As the top-floor apartment slowly rotated, he could look out over the whole city. *His* city.

He sat and sipped at his drink, watching the gathering storm approach the city. The lightning flashes and the thunderous rumbles kept him company. He played his childhood game of estimating the distance of the thunderhead based on the lag between flash and thunderclap. Summer storms were common, but they usually had little effect on the city, as it nestled beneath the escarpment of the Vantuba cliffs to the west and the sea to the north. Storms usually came in from the south and had lost their vigour by the time they arrived, but this one was coming from the north. It would be whipping up the sea, and the mountains would not have tempered its ferocity, so it would likely put on quite a show.

His wife was late. She was always late, and sometimes he wished that she was actually *late*. His chefs had a difficult job with his wife's punctuality. If they produced the dinner on time, it would be spoiled by his wife's tardiness, and if they were late, then she would, just out of badness, turn up on time, and then the pair of them would have to sit in awkward silence until the food appeared. They had been married for many years, some of them good, but he struggled to remember which ones.

"What's your poison tonight, KK?" said Myra as she entered the room and eyed the half-finished drink in his hand. The sentence mixed the nostalgic use of her pet name for him with an edge, suggesting its use was ironic.

"The usual, just more of it, My. You going to join me?" mirroring his wife's tone. He knew that she hated him calling her My. At least he hadn't called her my My. That would have probably left him eating alone.

"I'll have wine with the food."

"Storm coming…"

"There usually is, Kelvin—"

"How's Isabella?"

"Mother is old and full of spirit. 'Bit like you."

"The storm gathers pace," said Kelvin.

With initial and customary hostilities over, Myra sat down in the armchair opposite Kelvin. She didn't look at him but studied the gathering storm outside instead.

"Why are we like this?" Myra said, this time with no hint of bitterness.

"And when did we start being like this?"

"It was before…"

"I know.

"Before was bearable, but now…"

"I know."

"I wish we did."

"What?"

"Know. Know where she is, where she is, Kelvin! You have control of this enormous organisation. Hell, you basically control this city, and you cannot come up with anything about our missing daughter. Nothing from her and nothing from you."

An awkward silence descended, eventually broken by the arrival of the servant.

"Dinner is served, Mr Kraxler."

"Thank you. We will be in in a moment."

Myra remained in her chair, blankly looking out over the city.

"Come on. Let's eat. Then you will allow yourself some wine."

Kelvin took her hand and gently coaxed her out of her thoughts and towards dinner. When he looked at her now, he realised that she had aged ten years in the last five, and a missing daughter was not helping matters. He could still see flashes of the old Myra—the Myra from before. But the light had to catch her right. When they had first met, she had looked fantastic, whatever the light did.

They went through to dinner. He looked at his wife and wondered if he was morphing into his father, just as she was undoubtedly morphing into her mother.

"Have you heard from Connie or Leon this week?" ventured Kelvin.

"Connie is in the mountains."

"Leon?"

"Immersed in work. Work for you, so you already know that. We should meet up as a family when Connie gets back."

"They are adults and have their own lives, Myra." Kelvin tried to deflect the subject. Getting the family together would make the elephant in the room as visible as the missing Sienna would be invisible.

After a pause. "So what have you got Leon into at the moment?"

"He's investigating activity in Teath."

"What does that mean? Investigating?Activity? Teath is not safe. Is he there in person?"

"He wants to be hands-on. He wants some excitement. He is safe enough."

"He's with a team, right?"

"Yes. There are five of them. All capable of looking after themselves."

"Activity?"

"What?"

"What activity are Leon's hands on?"

"Illegal weapon imports into the city."

"So, completely safe then." She shoved her food around her plate, torn between sipping and gulping her red wine.

Kelvin thought, *Only women are capable of administering sarcasm in such a small, but lethal dose.*

"Myra, you can die crossing the street."

"You can go missing crossing the street." She opted for the gulp.

He joined her, knowing he just had to get through the meal. In all likelihood, his wife would depart to her private apartment, reducing the level of emotional torture considerably.

"Have you spoken to Connie?" He asked.

"Not this week. She likes the solitude of the mountains."

"Where is she?"

"Not sure, but she must be fine. She would get in touch if there were a problem."

"You still have the team looking for Sienna, don't you?"

"Of course I do, Myra. They are a permanent thing until we find her."

"They have found nothing. Maybe we should change that team and get help from outside the Kraxler Corporation."

"They are the best in the city, Myra."

"I know it's a cliché, but we need closure, Kelvin. I think I would rather actually find her body than not know. She could be anywhere. Imprisoned, tortured, whatever."

"Myra, we go over this constantly. I don't know what else to do."

"Fine. Maybe The Kraxler Organisation could worry more about what happened to Sienna than about illegal weapons coming into Tangreco."

"We still have to pay the bills, Myra. The company won't survive without that sort of work."

"Kelvin, you have more money than you can spend."

"Mr Kraxler. Excuse the interruption, but—" It was the servant again.

"What?"

"Mr Keogh is here to see you."

Without even a glance at his wife, Kelvin Kraxler told the servant to send him in.

"Elliott. Come in. Drink?" It sounded like an instruction.

"Not right now, Kelvin." He looked worried. "The storm has taken out the power at Vantuba Prison. The prisoners are all outside their cells in the main body of the prison. It seems that the backup generators failed—"

"No one has escaped?"

"No. Twenty armed surveillance drones are patrolling the perimeter."

"Can you get me the feed?"

"On the screen next door."

"I think I have just lost my appetite," said Myra. "I'm going to bed. Do something, Kraxler!"

Myra departed without another word and did not look at either man.

The men seemingly ignored her departure. They had other things to be concerned about.

Each drone feed showed a view of Vantuba prison. One view was directly over the prison's centre, showing the other drones slowly circling. Smoke was visible emanating from the top of the central dome. The feed did not have sound.

"Elliott. What options have we?"

"Armed operational team is en route. ETA: fifteen minutes. Any escapees will be easily found via their implanted locator beacons."

Kelvin turned away from the screen and looked out of the window. Through the rain, he could just about make out the clifftop prison in the distance, from which a faint red glow emanated.

Kelvin took the remains of his pre-dinner drink, topped it up, sat down, and watched the drone feed.

To his drink, Kelvin said, "I wonder if it's time for a more permanent solution. A more permanent solution regarding Victor Atkar,"

Elliott said, "Victor is—"

"Victor Atkar is a bad lot. We should be permanently rid of him. What has he done to Sienna? What has he done to Sam?" Kelvin said quietly.

"We don't know, do we? Kelvin, we don't even know if it was him who took them both."

"We know," Kelvin said, putting his arm around Elliott's shoulders.

22

Victor counted, but the storm's noise prevented him from hearing the splash below. There was no more from the chute either. Both men looked at each other.

"They will send help, Vic."

"Not for a while, Mr Moyes. It will take a while for the good guys to take back control and longer to assess losses."

"Losses?"

"Well, there are at least three. You, me, and your colleague who just reached terminal velocity. There will probably be more inside."

"We wait here, Vic. They will come for us eventually."

"There may be several days worth of food waste covering you before anyone thinks to look for you here. We can't go back up the chute. That leaves us with—"

"Climbing up the cliff or climbing down to the river," Luc interrupted.

"Do you know how high this cliff is, Mr Moyes?"

"About forty meters, I think."

"We are already about ten meters down. Thirty to go."

"No. We wait."

They waited, neither looking nor speaking to one another. The wind and rain gradually eased, and the darkness showed signs of relinquishing its command to the light of day. Their earlier frantic scampering and the heavy rain had cleared much of the platform of the slippery detritus.

"We have differing agendas, Mr Moyes," said Victor.

"True."

"You need to stay alive, and I need to stay alive and leave the prison. I have to get down the cliff."

"And I am supposed to stop you."

Victor did not reply but tentatively let go of the towel and slowly crawled to the cliff edge. Below, he could see the western branch of the Tangreco River, skirting the city boundary. The city districts of Maybyn and Breoc lifted themselves gradually from the river. He was on his hands and knees now, looking down the cliff face and the river below. He was distinctly unsure about the navigability of the cliff without the appropriate kit. He was distinctly unsure about a leap of faith. He was sure, though, that he would not stay and await reincarceration.

He got to his feet and backed up towards Luc, the cliff face rising above and behind them, Moyes still sitting.

"Long way down, Mr Moyes."

"You won't make it."

"No good options, Mr Moyes."

"Vic. You will get better treatment. You saved me in there. Every guard will know, know what you did for me. You may even get your sentence reviewed."

"Every guard and every prisoner will know Mr Moyes. No way will it get easier."

Victor gave him a quiet glance.

"No, Vic—"

Victor sprinted for his life. Six strides. Luc scrambled up to his hands and knees and failed miserably to grab at him.

"No, Vic—"

Victor was already over the cliff edge, dropping like a

stone towards the choppy waters of the Tangreco River.

Moyes reached the cliff edge. He could see the river below, but the light was still too dim to see any detail.

The pain was everywhere. After much mid-air flailing, he had hit the water, feet first. He knew from bitter experience that pain came in two guises. The fast pain of the impact was starting to fade, but the slow pain in the joints of his ankles, knees and hips was building rapidly. The pain in his chest, holding his breath, still beneath the river, was burning. He had timed his last gasp well, and his full chest was now carrying him upwards. He was too dazed to know which way was up, so he let the air in his chest do its work. Seconds seemed like minutes. He had to hang on, had to not fill his lungs with river water. As his head broke the surface, he exhaled. He was facing into the wind and took a wave of river water in the face just as reflex inhalation kicked in. Coughing and spluttering, he managed to make his body turn its back to the weather and waves. He should have done many things first, but Victor chose to look up at the cliff; the cliff that continued vertically for many meters below the water. The lifting gloom allowed him to see the top of the cliff, but he couldn't see Luc.

Victor managed to take a few breaths and returned his attention to river level. There was a large barge at anchor at the base of the cliff and a sailboat beyond that. His senses were returning now, but the pain in his legs was brutal. He used his arms to take him towards the craft. Eventually, he made it to the anchor chain of the barge and wrapped his arms around it. It was exhausting swimming with arms only, fully clothed. But he had always been strong, and there was little else to do in a cell than to train and keep fit. He took off his prison garb, wrapped the shoes inside and used the arms to tie the bundle to the links of the anchor chain. Now, in just his underwear, he could swim more freely. He circumnavigated the barge but could find no way out of the water. He would have to try for the sailboat or swim the whole width of the river. The boat option won out.

After several minutes of swimming, he reached the sailboat. He was grateful for the direction of the wind, which gave him shelter behind the stern. He was even more thankful for the ladder that the sloppy sailing owner had left dangling in the water. Searing pain through the soles of his feet and knees slowed his progress up the ladder and out of the water. Slowly, he dragged himself into the cockpit. There were no obvious signs of life on board, and the main hatch was closed but not locked.

Victor slid the hatch forward and peered inside. All seemed quiet as he went down below. The night was still dark, and the breaking dawn had yet to pierce the dim interior of the boat. He could just about make out the doors to the cabins, all of which were shut. He tried opening the port side aft cabin door, but it was locked. The same was true for the starboard side. He moved forward and gently tried the door of the fore cabin. It was not locked. He pushed the door gently forward and leaned his head into the cabin.

The blow struck him on the left side of his face, with most of the impact taken on his nasal bones. The back of Victor's head hit the bulkhead, and he dropped to the floor, only half intentionally. Lights came on as he tried to right himself. Still dazed, he found his arms tangled in a cargo net. Just as he made it back to his feet, two feet smashed into his gut, using it as a trampoline, flooring him again and taking the air from his sodden lungs. The feet's owner had leapt over Victor into the saloon, leaving him on the cabin floor.

"Why you on boat?"

Victor couldn't reply even if he'd wanted to. There was no air in his lungs. He gasped for some.

"Why you on boat?"

"I..., I..." Victor wheezed

"You off boat."

Blood was flooding out of Victor's nose and down the back of his throat. His left eye was already closing. Some air was now getting in, and his vision was getting the hang of the lighting.

"You off boat ." The face and voice came closer, but Victor's arms were still entwined in the netting.

"I..., I..." Victor was controlling the airflow better now, but he deliberately kept the struggle in his words.

The voice bent over him, wide eyes only inches from Victor's face.

"You off boat now. Or dead."

Victor's right leg kicked out and connected with the Voice's tender region between its legs. The Voice groaned and rolled forward towards Victor, putting out a hand to steady the fall. Victor rolled forward on top of the Voice, entangling his opponent in the netting and freeing himself. Whilst the Voice groaned, Victor secured the netting and tied the whole bundle to the door.

Victor sat back. His eye was now almost completely closed. His whole body ached.

"Clothes. Need clothes." Victor imitated his assailant's speech. "Where clothes?"

The Voice lifted his eyes to the overhead lockers but said nothing. Victor lifted himself up and opened the lockers. Soon, he was fully clothed and no longer in prison garb.

"Now, shoes." Again, the Voice just moved his eyes.

"Now food," said Victor.

Carefully, Victor stepped back from the netted boat owner. He took the food from the store and cooked it up in the

Galley. Without further altercation, both men shared the meal.

"What you want with boat?"

"You help me, you don't die."

"What you want with boat?"

"You take me upriver, I keep clothes, you don't die."

"You pay?"

"Later, for sure. I always pay my debts, but I can't pay you now."

There was silence for a few minutes as both men considered their positions. Victor couldn't sail a boat, and the other couldn't move.

"Okay. I take you Ervan docks. It quick. Wind and tide help now. You pay later, or I find you."

"Okay. Problems, I kill you," said Victor

"Okay. You not pay later, I kill you."

"Okay. What your name?"

"Call me boat name. Silver Ghost."

Victor tentatively released Silver Ghost from his entanglement, all the while ready to attack him again if he gave any trouble. Silver Ghost edged past him and climbed up on deck.

"I get small sail up. You help. Pull up anchor… It at pointy end." Victor watched Silver Ghost smile, though he couldn't work out what the smile meant.

Soon, the small head sail and the anchor were up. The Silver Ghost slid slowly around and headed up the river through the choppy, dark waters.

23

Sienna hated the magnificent view from the penthouse apartment in which her father's minions had incarcerated her. It felt like bacon frying in front of a hunger striker. Every morning, she left the blinds closed for as long as she could bear, until the artificial light became too much and she had to let the natural version in.

The days were long and tedious. There was an exercise suite, which she used to the point of exhaustion. Video entertainment was provided, which became somewhat repetitive. There was a news feed, which was also a bit repetitive and slightly more depressing. There was limited access to online content. There was social interaction with her guards at the door. This had become one of the highlights of her day. At least they were vaguely human. There was the kitchen, in which she experimented and cooked up some delightful meals for three. She fed the guards now on a regular basis. There was the drinks cabinet, filled and refilled with anything she wanted. She tried to keep away from it as much as possible. Bacon and hunger again.

For now, Sienna sat at a computer and explored online. She had managed to find some back doors to where she wanted to go, and the content watchers had become a lot less vigilant of late. Everyone got lazy in the end. She had managed to discover what had happened to Victor: the trial details, his incarceration in Vantuba Prison, and the fact that her father was one of the judges. The news feed droned on in the background.

She agonised constantly about any conceivable scenario in which her father would allow her to be released to tell her story. The answer in her mind was slightly clearer each day - he wouldn't. Why did he not just have her killed? Maybe there was a very small and reclusive conscience somewhere in his heart.

Time for a cook-up.

Sienna went to the kitchen and dived into the stores for inspiration for a late-night feast for her and her guards. The news feed from the city droned on. Droned on until she heard…

Tonight's storm has taken out the power at the Vantuba Prison. The latest information we have is that the prisoners are out of their cells and rioting. There is a fire raging in the prison.

Sienna shelved her cooking plans and listened to the news feed until she realised she would get no more information as the item had already started to repeat.

She went back to her computer and entered one of the software back doors. Soon she had a live video feed of the storm-ridden prison. The software she had been given to relieve her boredom now became invaluable. She ran the video through the software and zoomed in on two figures on a cliff top. Two figures and then only one.

24

Kelvin decided that watching the drone feed was a distinctly dehydrating experience.

"More drinks, please."

The servant hovering at the door departed on his mission.

Kelvin placed his empty crystal glass on the table. It rattled a little before coming to rest. He moved to his screen and zoomed in on the camera feeds. There was nothing much to see. Rain and cloud. Fire and smoke. No sign of people. More specifically, there is no sign of Atkar.

He continued watching as the servant reappeared with drinks for Kelvin and Elliott.

"It better be strong."

"I can make another."

Kelvin didn't answer immediately. His eye had caught something on one of the feeds. He downed the drink in a few gulps. "Yes, please. Strong and quick."

The servant left once more, and Kelvin tried depositing the second glass onto the table while his attention was on the feeds. He let it go prematurely, and it shattered on impact with the table. He did not even blink.

The servant returned and handed both men their drinks.

"Thank you. Can you see that, Elliott?" Can you rewind it

and zoom it in?"

Elliott moved forward, relinquished his drink, untouched, and obeyed both instructions.

Both men stood and watched the feed, which showed two men on a ledge within the cliff face below the prison. The men were dressed in dissimilar uniforms.

"A prisoner and a guard?" said Kelvin

"Looks that way."

"Back it up and enhance it. I want to know if it's him."

Silently, Elliott did as requested.

The two men watched the enhanced feed. The tremor in Kelvin's hand increased. "It's him! It's Atkar!"

"It's Victor," Elliott said quite quietly. The faintest of smiles crossed his face.

They watched as one of the men dropped into the river. Kelvin's new drink in its new glass dropped to the table, shattering like the last. It would be cleaned up later.

"Get the drones down to river level. I need the body found."

"We need to find Victor," Elliott said quietly again. Then, more loudly, "It will take a while to reprogram the drones. They are supposed to be watching the prison."

"Do it. And get some of our people there, too."

"We should alert medics. Victor might still be alive but injured." Elliott's voice displayed the slightest of tremors.

"Cody Warne. Get Cody on it. He is close by. I think it's time our friend Victor Atkar was more permanently dealt with, although he may be dead anyway. Warne can do that?"

"Victor lived as my son, along with Carlos. We need to find him."

Kelvin looked at Elliott and saw the problem.

"I want Victor Atkar found and dead, and Elliott wants him found and alive and well."

"Elliott. Get a drone there ASAP. We need to find Atkar

dead or alive, but we need to find him. Also, get Cody on the case. How long will it take to get a drone there?"

"The prison drones were on site. That's where this feed is coming from. A remote-controlled drone will take about thirty minutes to arrive and be set up, but it would struggle to locate him in these conditions. It would be better to use an A.I.D. programmed with his biometrics. It's a shame they are no longer legal," said Elliott in a strange tone.

"Okay. How long would it take to load biometrics and to task an Artificial Intelligence Drone with a mission regarding Atkar... theoretically?"

"Probably a few hours. Even if we had his biometrics to hand—"

"We do."

"We would still need to task the AID, which we don't have —"

"We do."

"We do?"

"Or rather, we can. I have some interesting items stored here in the city. Some right here in this building. Some are under the wing of 'Mr Cody Warne.' He may become busier than he expected tonight."

"Do we have someone who could load the mission algorithms and biometrics?"

"Search, locate and destroy ?" Kelvin said in a strange tone.

"Search, locate and rescue. Not many people around who can do it now. If you want to keep it close, then use your son. He could do it" Elliott said.

"Leon is in Teath with his team..."

"They could pick it up direct from Warne. The quickest way would be by boat."

Kelvin thought for a moment. "Okay, Elliott, let's get it sorted. Oh, and get a remote-controlled drone down there

ASAP, anyway. We may be lucky to find Atkar before using the AID. Also, get some automated drones to chase Atkar's locator beacon. I will contact Leon and Warne personally."

The servant started to clean the broken glass and whiskey.

Kelvin just looked at him. "Later! That will keep."

Elliott rose, nodded and left without another word. He would call Leon to clarify the mission after Kelvin's call. Changing "destroy" for something less final.

Kelvin picked up his phone and returned to watch the video feeds of the prison. Then, he called his son.

"Leon. You free for a bit of excitement?"

"You got me chasing down the competition. Has something else come up?"

"Get you and your team to Cody's place. He is looking after a bit of kit for us at the moment, and we need it now. It's an AID."

"No!"

"Yes - and you will need to load everything it needs."

"But—"

"But nothing. This is top of our list now. I know you can do it."

"I've never done it before! I've read about it, but that's all."

"Exactly the same as sex the first time, then. I'm sure you knew all about that in theory before putting it into practice for the first time. I'm hoping that extending the metaphor might also mean that it won't take you very long. Stop everything else and get the thing from Warne and bring it here."

"Okay. Straight on it."

Kelvin cut the call and dialled Cody.

He made several other calls. Wheels were in motion.

After the call, he relaxed a little. Wheels were in motion. All would be well.

25

Ervan Docklands was an import and export hub for the city and a haven for shipping. Even monster craft could navigate the deep channel under the Vantuba cliff face to get to the docks. Sea views were lacking, however, which detracted from the waterfront and precluded any prospect of well-to-do housing popping up. It had remained a poor area since the city's early days, unlike the waterfronts of Erth, whose inhabitants had sea views and money.

The Silver Ghost tied up alongside the run-down, empty jetty.

"Job done," said Silver Ghost

"Come with me, and I will pay you," said Victor

"You no money."

"I pay my debts. Let's go and see if others do the same."

"Not tricks?"

"No tricks," confirmed Victor, gently correcting his companion's choice of words.

They left the boat and wandered along the pontoon.

"You face look bad."

Victor didn't need telling. His eye was almost completely closed, making a reasonable effort at appearing like an aubergine trying to escape his face. "Follow me," he said.

He kept his head down as they walked. His objective was about a five-minute walk away through a maze of steel containers.

Victor, with the sailor just behind him, arrived at a door above which was written, "You have been WarneD!" Victor pushed the door and went inside. The armed man eyed them up and down.

"Mr Atkar for Mr Warne," announced Victor

No movement from the guard.

"And I know he's in the office. He's always in the office, and now would be very convenient for us both."

The guard remained seated but reached behind himself and rapped on the door three times. The inner guard opened the door and examined the outer guard and the guests.

"Mr Atkar for Mr Warne. Last time,"

The door briefly closed and then reopened. The inner guard motioned them forward. They entered the room, and the door behind them closed. A door ahead of them opened, and in strode Mr Cody Warne.

"You're not looking too good, Victor."

"I could be looking a lot worse."

"Who is your friend?"

"More of a recent acquaintance. Mr Ghost, meet Mr Cody Warne."

Warne gave a brief nod. "What can I do for you, Mr Atkar?"

"Debt repayment, I think."

Warne gave a much slower, more contemplative nod. "Well —"

"Well, to be fair, I don't think you were expecting to repay for a while yet, so the money can wait. What I need now is for your people to remove my locator beacon."

"Or, we could just not do that and turn you in."

"That would greatly improve your reputation on the

streets, Cody."

"I will get someone to fix it for you this afternoon. Would you two like breakfast?"

"Eaten," said the voice behind Victor. Silver Ghost seemed to be getting the hang of the situation.

"Within the hour would be a great improvement on that and will reduce the interest rate on what you owe me."

Warne nodded to the inner guard. "Go and get Mike now. He will need his usual kit."

They were left alone.

"I also need some hardware."

"Top-end stuff, I assume? It will be expensive."

"Do you know how much you owe me? Still gambling, Cody? I also need the items within the next hour. You will have it safely stashed away in one of your containers. It won't be a problem. Find out where the hardware is, and we will get it now while we wait for Mike."

Warne looked pale, turned to the screen before him, and ordered the hardware he knew Victor wanted.

"Thirty minutes. Efficient—"

"When you want to be Cody. Nice slogan over the door, too. Please tell me you didn't pay someone to make that up for you. One more thing, Cody. I will need a small amount of working capital."

Silver Ghost backed towards the door and away from Victor, who stood over Cody's desk. More options in case of any trouble. The door opened, and a man carrying a kit bag strode in.

"Mike," said Cody, gesturing by way of introduction. "This is an old acquaintance of mine. Victor Atkar. And we need a favour. Please remove his locator beacon."

"That's not a good plan. As soon as a locator beacon is removed from the body, it pings base camp, flagging up its location and the fact that it has been removed. So if we do it here, they will know we removed it. They will have people all over us in minutes."

"Cody, you are repaying your debts quite rapidly this morning. You must have a fast boat. It can take us down the river to—"

"No. You can go from here with Mike until you are far enough away that we will not be implicated or descended on. Then we will pick you up by fast, untracked boat and take you anywhere on the three rivers."

"The plan is good. Where will the boat pick us up?" said Victor

"Piran Park will be quiet before lunch. I can remove the LB there and meet the boat on Piran Pier," suggested Mike.

"Okay. If this works, Cody, you can consider yourself nearly done with debt repayment. Silver Ghost here needs some cash payment for his troubles today. Then that's it."

"I will sort him out," said Warne.

"No. I think I go Victor,"

"No. Cody Warne will pay you for today."

"But I pay you for your eye," said Silver Ghost.

"No need. Just one thing, though. What is your real name?"

"Posnanski," said Silver Ghost.

"Thanks for the ride this morning, Posnanski. The eye will mend soon enough, and Cody here will pay you before you leave." Victor held out his right hand. Posnanski did likewise, and they shook as if to celebrate a good morning's work. They nodded their farewells.

"Just waiting for the MFB and the other stuff, Cody, then I will be out of your hair."

"Go. I will arrange for it to get to you at Piran Park. And it's Mr!"

"Pay Posnanski, and he will be out of your hair, too."

Cody did not reply, and the inner guard closed the door

behind Victor and Mike.

26

Cody sat behind his desk and seemed to drift off into his own world, looking at his feet. He did not look relaxed. He didn't like what he was seeing. Anything involving Atkar might prove to be complicated. Victor's sudden reappearance was extremely troubling. At least he had got him to leave without any payment. He knew he would be back unless he supplied him with the costly multifunction bulb. They were scarce now after decades of being banned by the authorities.

His intercom rang, bringing him back to reality. "Who wants me now?"

"Mr Kelvin Kraxler on the phone," from the intercom.

Slightly flustered, Cody replied, "Put him through, you idiot."

He lifted his eyes just before opening his mouth and saw Posnanski standing beside the door.

"Mr Kraxler, what—"

"Cut the bullshit politeness... Mr Warne." Kelvin combined aggression with irony.

Cody knew very well that his full attention was needed on this call. He also wanted it private. Posnanski showed no sign of moving. Warne could do without a performance while on the call.

"Leon is on his way to make a collection," said Kelvin.

"A collection of what Mr Kraxler?"

"The item number is PJ07011927."

Just a moment, Mr Kraxler. I need to note the number. It might take a bit of time."

Kelvin repeated it slowly as if talking to an infant.

"Read it back to me so there are no mistakes."

Cody did so.

"When—" said Warne, but Kelvin had already hung up.

Cody yelled at his men. "Get him out of here. Then get me—"

"You suppose pay me," said Posnanski.

Warne did not reply, but he looked at two of his men and then back to Posnanski.

Warne's men were slightly hesitant but had no option but to approach Posnanski. Just as they did so, he raised his hands in submission. "Debts will be paid."

"Get out of my office," said Warne, waving a finger at Posnanski.

Warne held out a slip of paper to his men. "You two get this from Mr Kraxler's store. No cock ups and rapidly, please."

Once outside Warne's office, Posnanski headed back toward the wharf. Looking over his shoulder, he saw the backs of his guardians departing into the compound. Once they were out of sight, Posnanski turned and followed, ducking into one of the openings between the containers, quietly entering Warne's storage area. He did not like not being paid when promised.

27

Victor wondered if his name really was Mike. He was leading the way along the riverbank road from the Ervan dock yard towards the Piran area of the city. This river branch was much calmer than the one Victor had entered from a great height earlier. The city's buildings sheltered it from the northerly gale, and the storm was abating too. The rain had stopped.

"What's in the bag?" asked Victor.

Mike turned to him. His look indicated a deep reluctance to talk, and he turned away again without reply.

Victor was in no mood for such things. "What's in the bag?" he repeated.

Still silence. They walked on. The road and river were quiet, with most taking the storm as an excuse to stay out of the elements.

"What's in the bag?" Victor asked again, and again there was no reply.

Without appearing to break stride, Victor placed his left leg directly in front of Mike and swung him around it. In the same movement, he grabbed his shoulders and continued the rotation. Mike found his face pressed into the rough road surface and one arm trapped beneath his body. Victor's right knee pressed on his neck.

"Shall we try again, because I am a little time-constrained? What's in the bag?"

"My surgical kit - to remove your locator beacon," wheezed Mike.

"Open it for me." Pressure increasing on his neck.

"But—"

"Open it now."

Mike managed to swing his left arm forward so that the bag was in front of his face. "I need to use both hands," pleaded Mike.

"How about one hand each?

"But—"

"Let's try it and see."

Victor adjusted his weight so that he could just about reach the bag and keep Mike pinned to the road.

"Hold the bag still, Mike, and I will unzip it."

The pain in his face and neck left Mike with no option other than to comply with Victor's request. Victor slowly unzipped the bag and tilted the opening towards himself to inspect its contents.

"Here we go, Mike. Sterile pouch with surgical kit. Gun—"

"If you kill me, then the locator beacon remains inside you, tracing your movements. You will be tracked down within the day."

Victor took the gun and zipped up the bag.

"I'll have the bag now, Mike," he said quietly. A little more neck pressure soon proved adequate to entice Mike to release his grip. Victor checked the immediate area and could see no one. He moved the bag out of Mike's reach, patted him down in search of other weapons, and then grabbed the bag again. He rose to his feet, putting more pressure on Mike's neck just to make a point.

"I—"

"Don't worry. The job is only half done. Come on." Victor

explained.

Victor carried the bag in one hand while the other held the gun to Mike's side. Down the river, he could see the rendezvous point, Piran Pier.

"A little detour is in order," Victor guided Mike left, off the main riverside thoroughfare, towards the more built-up area within the Breoc district of the city. The rain had now stopped, but the sky remained overcast.

"What do you want?"

"I want what your boss implied would be done. I want my locator beacon removed."

They entered a small square with a few benches in the centre. Again, no one was around.

"Here is your operating theatre, Mike. Sit down, and we will get on with it."

"But once it's out of the body for a few minutes, it will raise an automatic alarm," said Mike.

"Let's start. It's on the inner side of my forearm. Just under the skin." Victor handed over the bag and extended his arm, while keeping the gun gently making its presence felt in Mike's side.

"Do you want local?" Mike asked—a slight tremor in his voice.

"Speed is much more important than lack of pain. Get on with it."

Mike looked at him and grabbed a scalpel blade from his kit. Then, he looked down at it and then back at Victor.

"Don't even think about it, Mike. Do whatever you need to remove the thing from my arm."

Mike made a small incision, put the scalpel down and picked up the mosquito surgical clips.

"Now would be good before I change my mind about you," Victor said, through a grimmace.

Mike cut further into Victor's arm. The blade touched the

LB, and Mike teased the thing out with the mosquito clip.

"I've got it—" Mike exclaimed.

"Stop! Now you."

"What?"

"Now you. Make a small incision in your arm and a hole to take the beacon."

"No way am I having your locator in me!"

The gun prodded into his side as a prompt.

"No local," said Victor

Mike's right hand shook as his scalpel hovered over the skin of his left forearm. The blade, bloodied from Victor's arm, touched the skin.

"Stop!" said Victor. "Change of plan."

Mike needed no encouragement to not make an incision in his own arm.

"If you don't want to cut into yourself, you can swallow it instead."

"Let me have it in my hand. You ever seen one before?" said Victor

"No."

"Put it in my hand."

The LB dropped into Victor's open palm, and he closed his fist around it.

"Swallow it or put it in your arm," Victor instructed.

Mike looked panic-stricken at the prospect of either option and started to turn away.

"The easy option was there for you. I don't have time for indecision," Victor said.

The gun was still pressing against Mike's side, but Victor's other hand, the one clenched into a fist around the LB, moved upwards at speed and connected with Mike's jaw, sending his head upwards and backwards. Mike hit the surface of the road as consciousness left him. Victor's arms cushioned the blow. No back of the skull implosion. Just a temporary blackout. Victor pocketed the gun, lifted the scalpel and plunged it deep into Mike's forearm. There wasn't much blood to start with. He pressed the LB into the wound opening, like stuffing a clove of garlic into a joint of meat for roasting. Gently at first, then more forcefully, he pushed hard with his index finger, plunging the LB deep into the muscle tissue. He lifted Mike onto the bench, snatched the medical bag and left Mike, looking for all the world like a sleeping drunk. Victor suspected he would be out for some time. Time enough for him to fashion a makeshift dressing for his arm wound.

Victor took the back streets towards Piran Park. Once at the park, he sauntered through the place with an unconcerned air. The park was a five hundred meter strip of green bordering one of the stream-sized tributaries of the Tangreco River. He followed the stream towards the river and towards the arranged rendezvous of Piran Pier. He needed the promised multi-function bulb, the MFB. The day was brightening as dawn changed to morning—the clouds higher and the wind lower. City folk had begun to venture out now that the storm had passed. He couldn't see anyone on the pier. Cody's courier would be looking for two men. Alone, he didn't fit the bill. He was confident, though, that he could spot a courier easily enough.

Patience, Victor, patience. It could be that Cody was having difficulty acquiring the MFB.

Victor walked slowly towards the edge of the park. He heard them before he saw them. When he did see them a few seconds later, his concern grew. He could see boats approaching from the east. They were black, sleek and fast. They looked to be heading to Piran Pier.

Shit!

Victor could think of only one explanation. Cody must have double-crossed him. It also meant he would not be sourcing the hardware he needed from Cody either.

Priorities were now different. First, don't get caught, then sort out the long-term issues. He took off his coat and turned it inside out. Now, he looked like a war zone. Blood from his arm was all over the sleeve, and his eye was black and blue. He decided that walking directly away from the pier might attract attention and possibly the attention of automated drones, so he walked parallel to the river. The boats continued to approach. He reached the park's edge, retracing his earlier steps, heading back towards Ervan dockyard. Hopefully, any search would concentrate on someone heading east, away from Ervan. He slowly headed west. He did not turn to check on events behind him in case he was spotted. The boat engine noise was getting louder. It seemed like they must be almost upon him. Suddenly, they zoomed past him, heading upriver towards the main channel and Ervan's docks without slowing.

Victor did not break stride, still concerned about drones tracking the Locator Beacon. He took a right and headed into the city's depths, away from the river. He needed to be off the streets now. The brightening day was definitely darkening his prospects.

28

Mike slowly became aware of the pain. There was pain in his jaw. There was pain in his neck, and there was pain in his arm. He opened his eyes slowly, taking in his surroundings. The memory of his pre-unconscious state was gradually overtaken by the present and more pressing state in which he found himself. He tried to lift himself from the bench. He managed it, despite severe pain in his neck. He tried to support himself, seated on the bench. More pain, this time searing through his arm, as he tried to get to his feet. He looked down to see the stab incision and bruising of his forearm. He knew what it meant. Inside his arm resided the fugitive's locator beacon. They would be tracking him, not Victor.

I need to get it out of my arm! I need my medical kit.

He looked around and realised he was without anything he could use. He had more instruments at home and at the office. The office and Cody did not appeal right now. He could hear drones in the distance. They were getting closer, for sure.

Are they chasing me and the locator, or Victor Atkar?

He headed out from the park and into the nearest subway station. He headed down towards the platforms. Hopefully, the drones would not be able to track him below ground. He didn't know if they could. A train would outpace them anyway. The priority now was to get on any train. The passenger barrier was open, and he easily got onto a platform. A subway train was approaching. He managed to get onto the train and find an empty carriage, and he slumped into a seat just as the doors closed. The train started to pull away, heading for the tunnel, and he began to relax a little.

The drone appeared at his window, matching the train's velocity. He saw the barrel under the drone rotate towards him, and he dropped to the floor in a vain attempt to hide. The drone was obviously on a kill mission, not a capture mission. As he hit the carriage floor, a huge crash occurred, and glass splintered over him. The drone and the carriage had both tried to enter the tunnel together. In the confined space, the rotor blades had smashed through the window into the carriage, leaving the drone's body to fall to the tunnel floor.

They are chasing me, and underground is no cover!

He was back on the seat as the train continued into the tunnel. He braved the agony and plunged his fingertips into the wound in his forearm. He had to get the locator beacon out, or he would be a dead man. He could feel the tip of it, but couldn't gain any purchase. He just kept pushing it deeper into the muscle. Desperate now, he looked overhead and smashed the glass covering the overhead lighting. He pulled the light from its socket and tugged at the wires beneath. Eventually, he managed to release one of the wires and fashion it into a hook, which he plunged into his arm. He nearly passed out with the pain, sweat running into his eyes. He could feel the wire hook over the other side of the bean-shaped death trap within the muscle. Delicately, he tried to pull the thing to the surface, but the suction within the tissues was holding it in place. He kept at it, pain searing through his mind, and eventually, the locator popped out onto the floor of the carriage. He bent over and picked it up. The next station was approaching fast. As the train pulled in, he knew he must part company with the thing. Either he or the locator beacon was leaving the train at the station. The train pulled in, and he jumped off it. He moved along the platform and deliberately bumped into one of the other passengers leaving the train, slipped the locator into the hood of her jacket and headed back to the subway train. He just managed to get through the sliding doors before they closed.

As the train picked up speed, he started to relax again. He watched the other passenger enter the stairwell. As his train entered the tunnel, he just caught a glimpse of the passenger slumping backwards onto the platform with a large hole in her chest. A drone hovering over the scene. He felt a pain in his chest now—an acidic fear pressing down on him. Behind him in the station, a panicked public swirled on the platform. Screams of disbelief and fear reached his departing carriage before it was swallowed into the darkness.

29

The storm outside was receding, but the one inside her was intensifying.

Victor was out!

She was not out!

Outside her apartment door, there was a constant presence. Whenever she looked through the peephole in the door, there was at least one guard; most of the time, there were two. They rarely troubled her. They only entered the apartment if she was in danger, obviously up to no good, or she had cooked for them out of boredom. They brought her the items she had requested and removed things she no longer wanted around.

The guards were like secure housekeepers who had instructions that needed to be adhered to.

There should always be two guards at the apartment. Do not let any harm come to the occupant. Get her whatever she needs. Never enter the apartment unaccompanied.

But Sienna had not given any problems for ages, and the guards had started taking a slightly less rigorous view of the instructions. The occasional lapse had become almost routine, often with only one of the guards remaining outside, monitoring her. Today's guards were brothers. Philip and John. Philip took the job seriously, and John took it less so. John often took a break on the street for a smoke and a chat with anyone passing by.

Sienna checked the peephole and discovered only Philip outside.

She decided to take a bath. She undressed, wrapped a large, luxurious towel around her slender body, and started to fill the bath. The drinks cabinet was her next target. She grabbed the full bottle of vodka and placed it on the edge of the bath in full view of the security camera. Once the bath was full, she dropped the towel and slid into the steaming water, grabbing the bottle as she went. The camera gave the guards, if they wanted it, a pretty good view of the right side of the naked Sienna. Bathtime usually had the guards at their most attentive. She made a show of drinking from the neck of the vodka bottle. The camera feed showed her drinking the spirit, but the bottle opening was only close to her lips. The clear spirit slipped gently into the water. Sienna and the bottle then did the same. She waited motionless, with her ears and nostrils just above the water's surface and her eyes closed. She controlled her breathing. Not even a ripple showed on the water's surface.

Philip checked the monitor, and his adrenaline rush began. Absolutely never go into the apartment unaccompanied. He had no choice, though. He was alone, and Sienna was unconscious, or worse, in the bath. There was no doubt in his mind that if Sienna ended up dead, then so would he. He grabbed his pass key and entered the apartment. He sprinted along the hallway into the living area, into the bedroom, and then burst through the door to the bathroom. Sienna heard his approach, and she held her breath. Philip, shaking, bent over and felt for a pulse at Sienna's neck.

The Vodka bottle, filled with water, hit him in the right temple and smashed. He slumped over her as she tried to lift herself out of the water, his face transiently in an often dreamed-of position. She escaped the water with some shallow cuts on her belly. Philip's face remained beneath the now pink bathwater. She quickly dried herself and examined her cuts. Superficial and not too bad.

Shall I leave him to drown?

She struggled with the limp body but managed to flop him out onto his back. The back of his head hit the marble floor with a dull thud. She, with some difficulty, undressed him. Soon she was dressed as him and had grabbed all his kit. Her long red hair was problematic, but she tied it up as best she could.

Get out. Get out as quickly as possible.

Despite her thoughts of safety, she returned to check on Philip.

"Shit! Shit! Shit!" Sienna shouted to the room.

She once again grabbed his shoulders and shook him. "Wake up!"

Dead!

Now, I really must run.

Remorse mingled with a rising panic.

Finally, she found herself outside the apartment. She closed the apartment door and headed along the corridor. With Philip's bits safely grabbed, she accessed the service elevator and descended to the basement car lot without interruption.

Sienna was torn. Get out of the building and away as soon as possible, or try to grab some transport to get her further away. Trying not to run, she headed towards the exit ramp. She turned the last corner and onto the incline to the street. The smell of the rain, dirt, oil, and air was a heady mixture after the sterile air conditioning of the apartment. The urge to run became an irresistible subconscious drive to survive. Halfway up the ramp, she saw John heading down towards her. Unable to bluff it out, Sienna turned and ran back towards the relative safety of the car lot. John followed at a slower, but increasing pace. He tried to contact his uncontactable brother.

Sienna sprinted to the elevator, which hadn't moved since she left it. She pressed the call button, and the doors opened. She then pressed the button again to take her back up to the apartment. At the last moment, she changed her mind, backed out of the elevator and headed for the stairwell.

As John reached the elevator, there was no sign of Sienna. The floor level indicator displayed its smooth ascent through the building towards the top floor. With trembling hands, he tried to phone Philip and, just for a moment, thought he heard the ring.

As stealthily and as quickly as she could, Sienna ascended the stairs to street level. John kept at it with the phone and watched as the elevator reached the top floor. He pressed the call button. The elevator started its downward journey. After what seemed like an eternity, it reached the basement, and the doors opened on the empty interior. He got in, pressed the button for the top floor, and rode the elevator back to the penthouse apartment. Exiting the elevator, he could see that the apartment door was slightly ajar and that there was no sign of his brother.

"Phil?" he said as he approached the door.

He checked the camera feed, which revealed the aftermath in the bathroom.

"Phil!"

John barged the door full open and ran to his semi-naked, prostrate brother. There was blood in the water and a much more ominous pool of blood around Philip's head.

Philip's chest was motionless.

"Phil!" John shook his brother by the shoulders and plaintively called his brother's name once more. "Phil."

John sank to his knees, and the tears flowed silently down his cheeks. He got to his feet and went into the penthouse bedroom, pulled off the covers and used them to cover the body. Silently, he left the apartment. A steely resolve now replaced the fun and humour that normally inhabited his eyes.

30

With each passing minute, Victor felt safer. No drones were following him, and nobody was following him. He headed deep into the city, his head dancing with alternatives. His logical brain was trying to overcome his emotional one, and failing. Anger at the double-crossing Cody was building with every pace. Without even realising it, he had taken a route west into Breoc. It was a rejuvenated area for the most part. Only its southern tip was left poor and rundown. He broke his stride and stopped. There were just a few people about, but it was mostly quiet. When he eventually realised that he had been unconsciously heading back towards Cody, his thoughts crystallised. He would deal with the Warne issue first. Stealthily, he headed toward the landward boundary of Warne's compound. There was a high fence topped with razor wire. Like the containers beyond, it did not look new or well-maintained.

Victor tested the fence. It was mostly secure, but at ground level, animal digging had undermined it in some places. One defect was big enough to let Victor through. He crawled under the wire and made it inside.

You might regret a little lack of investment, Mr Warne.

He scrambled away from the fence towards the containers.

Slowly and circuitously, he made his way towards Warne's office. It was uncannily quiet. He was beginning to worry that Warne had left when he suddenly heard voices and the noise of one of the containers being opened.

"This is the one."

"Where is the stuff? We haven't opened this container before."

"I have, but not for years. Come on. Warne wants this stuff ASAP. I think it's stuff for Kraxler."

Victor moved closer. The two men were inside the container now. Both doors were wide open but not folded back against the sides. Victor hid behind one of the doors and listened.

"Come on. The boss wants this quickly."

"Yeah, but he wants the right stuff, so let's make sure we don't muck up."

Victor slowly pushed on the door. It slowly and surprisingly quietly rotated towards the closed position. The other door was inexplicably doing the same thing.

"Hey, stop messing. We got a job to do here." Came from within.

Victor pushed at the door. Both the doors closed. Victor looked across at the unexpected force closing the other door and sealing Warne's men inside. Initially taken aback, he regained his wits and extended his right hand in a gesture of friendship.

"Silver Ghost! Posnanski! I thought you had gone." They clasped hands.

"I wait payment."

"So am I. We will take payment, I think, rather than waiting for it to be given."

Both men slowly opened their respective doors just a little, allowing a slender shaft of light to shed into the container.

"Stop fucking around, you guys! We need to see what

we're doing. It will be us in trouble with the boss, not you."

The two outside kept the doors open to about the width of a man. They had not discussed it. They had not planned it. They just both knew.

The crosser man came out through the slightly ajar doors and saw no one. He looked behind the door to his left. The punch to his jaw arrived a moment after recognition and before any exclamation. Victor caught the slumping body and laid it quietly on the ground. Posnanski was already inside the container. The other man inside was crouched down, looking into boxes. He turned and met the same fate as the other of Warne's men.

"They were after stuff for Kraxler," said Posnanski.

Victor said nothing but grabbed the note from the unconscious man. The items Warne wanted were in this container. They would not be getting to Kraxler any time soon.

"Keep watch," said Victor, "while I find our payment."

Both of Warne's men were still unconscious when Victor emerged from the container carrying three packages. He placed them at Posnanski's feet.

"Let me see that." Posnanski said.

He checked the stuff over.

"Good enough for shared payment, I think?" Posnanski said.

Between them they made the unconscious comfortable on the container. They closed and locked the doors.

"Can we take the payment to the Silver Ghost?"

"Yes. No fighting this time," said Posnanski. "What about men?"

"Leave them be. They were only doing their job, and not very well," said Victor.

Both men smiled as they stealthily made their way around the perimeter of Warne's compound to the wharf. They boarded the Silver Ghost without challenge. Victor took the packages down below whilst Posnanski made a deliberate show of putting the sails up and casting off. He even waved a goodbye to some of Warne's men, who had finally noticed the activity on the boat.

The one sail, two men and three packages, slipped away silently from the dockside and headed downstream towards Teath and the open sea. They glided past the fast boats tied up further along the dock. Men in dark outfits, guns slung over their shoulders, occupied the jetty.

"We need to get somewhere quiet to examine these things," said Victor

"I know where," Posnanski said.

During the crossing, Victor slept in the relative warmth of the cabin. Posnanski sailed the boat effortlessly. He watched the sails and constantly made adjustments, keeping them filled to provide maximum speed to their destination.

After four hours sailing into the weakening northerly breeze, the Silver Ghost arrived at the White Islands. The anchor and sails were dropped.

The islands were uninhabited. More correctly, they were pretty much uninhabitable. A fluke of wind and ocean currents had built the islands from floating plastic detritus. The sun had bleached them white. The plastic retained no fresh water; as a result, nothing much grew there, and few people wanted to go there.

"They will probably find us here eventually," said Victor.

"Safe for now. Will not find us if we not here. Is there safe place in city? Easy hide in a city." Posnanski said.

"Maybe. After we check our payments from Mr Cody Warne." Victor's voice was little more than a whisper.

31

John stood up and headed for the apartment door. His brother was dead, and he was as good as dead himself unless he found Sienna pretty damn quick. It wasn't easy, but he needed to work it out. Who killed his brother, and where was Sienna? Two things swirled in his head, mixing and mingling.

Damage limitation.

Revenge.

He rewound the last few minutes in his head. Sienna was dressed in Phil's clothes and had taken the elevator back up to this floor. Then he realised that he hadn't, in fact, seen Sienna get into the elevator.

She had taken the stairs. She was out on the street. He was a fool. Where would she go?

He dialled his boss on his way to the stairwell. He had to check it out even though he was sure she was long gone.

"We have a serious problem." He groaned.

"What?"

"My brother is dead, and Kraxler is no longer in the penthouse."

"Where is she?"

"Gone."

"Are you injured? Are you still in the game?"

"Yes and no." He lied. No, and yes, was the truth.

"Bad!" Exclaimed his boss, as if addressing a wayward canine.

The line went dead.

John knew that his boss, would have to call his boss, which would not be easy.

John rushed down the stairwell floor by floor. He got to street level and decided to continue to the bottom anyway. He drew a blank and raced back up to street level. No sign of her. He would need help. He would need help to keep out of reach of Kelvin Kraxler, and he would need help to find the bitch who had killed his brother.

32

Sienna tried to keep her adrenaline in check. She wanted to run, but anyone who ran down any city street attracted attention, and that she did not want. The storm had passed, and the sky was beginning to lighten. She needed somewhere safe to go. Somewhere off the street and somewhere the family would not think to look.

Carlos. It had to be Carlos. He would keep her safe until a sensible plan could be made. She walked along the river's west bank, heading south away from the sea and the well-to-do homes and offices that overlooked the sea and river mouth. She reckoned it would take a good hour to walk to the rejuvenated Minver docklands where Carlos had his apartment, if he was still there after all this time. She crossed the Arnac Bridge over the river to the east bank. The bridge was a high-arching structure spanning the wide part of the estuary. The brisk walk up the arch took some of the adrenaline out of her system, but she again found it difficult not to break into a trot on the downward side. The riverside path was typically well-kept, but this morning, it was covered in detritus blown in by the storm. She silently passed city workers beginning the cleanup. They didn't even glance at her.

She kept to the riverside as the city began to wake, rounding the long curve that would take her towards Minver and, hopefully, some safety. She had only been to Carlos's apartment once, and she worried that she wouldn't be able to find it.

The day was brightening as she approached the Minver dockland development. Her potential haven was not too far away now. She walked up and down the cloned streets with their cloned buildings. She couldn't remember the place that well. It was a nearly impossible task, but she could think of nothing else to do. Suddenly, her eye was drawn to one of the balconies overlooking the street. The curtains were drawn, and no lights were on, but on the balcony itself, there stood a stone statue of an angel. She remembered it. She had made fun of Carlos for keeping such a crass object.

She headed for the door, rang the entry bell next to the label marked C.A., and prayed that he would answer.

Nothing. She tried again. Still nothing. One more time. What could hurt? If he wasn't in, what would it matter if she kept her finger on the buzzer? She did, out of desperation as much as anything else. Eventually, she gave up and walked away from the doorway. She gave one last glance up to the balcony and tried to hold back the tears of frustration. As she blinked them back, she saw the curtain move. She stood motionless, looking up in full view of the furtive occupant. Then she went back and leaned on the buzzer again. Someone was in the apartment—friend, foe, or Carlos. Someone would come. She was almost past caring which it would be.

The entry lock clicked open. Sienna took her finger from the buzzer and launched herself through the door before it relocked. She started up the stairs to the first floor.

Carlos stood at his door with a concerned expression. He looked nothing like his brother, who was shaven-headed and blue-eyed. Carlos was dark-haired and had facial hair that was not well-kept.

"Sienna!"

"Carlos. Let me in! Let me in! I need your help."

"Go in. Go in. Where have you been?"

Sienna went into the apartment ahead of Carlos.

"Please help me, Carlos. I need a shower and clean clothes. Look at these. We will need to burn them or dump them. Could you please get me something else to wear? I don't care if they are yours or belong to one of your girlfriends or boyfriends. Where is Victor?"

"Where have you been?"

"High above this city. In a penthouse prison. Lovely views don't make up for the solitary confinement."

"Who—"

"I can't go back to that. Whatever happens, I cannot go back to that."

"Why—"

"Please let me shower and find me some clothes. Where is Victor? I need to see him. I think I have done something terrible."

"The shower is through there. I will find some clothes."

33

Cody was struggling with his day. The call from Kelvin demanding his items from the secure containers, followed by the utterly unexpected arrival of Victor, had put him off balance. Two seemingly unrelated things could not be coincidental.

He was pacing around, fractiously waiting for the items to be brought to him. The door to his office opened unannounced, and in strode four men in dark gear and carrying automatic weapons.

"We thought we would save you the trouble of summoning a courier, Cody."

"Leon! How nice to see you."

"And you, such a stickler for etiquette. Mr Kraxler will do. Where is the stuff?"

"It's on its way. Five minutes max."

Cody's mind helplessly went sideways.

He's going to be pissed off that I called him Max.

It was a fleeting and pointless thought. He turned to his men in the room and said, "Go and chase them up. They should be back by now."

The two men left.

"Busy morning, Mr Warne?"

"Routine, Mr Kraxler." Cody couldn't quite keep the sarcasm out of his words.

"So, other than our unexpected visit, nothing out of the ordinary?"

"Every day brings surprises." Warne played for time.

"Only for the unprepared."

"Even the best prepared can be surprised." Warne kept his tone deliberately neutral and non-confrontational.

"Let's hope there are no surprises today, then."

Silence hung in the air. As the seconds ticked by, the tension in Warne's body grew. It showed.

When Warne's office door opened, four of his men came in. Two, the recently departed, looked just a little smug. The other two, looking battered, seemed only to want to look at the floor.

"We found them in Mr Kraxler's container. Well, locked in Mr Kraxler's contain—"

"And the items?" interrupted Leon coldly.

"They took them," said one of the men.

"Who took them?" Leon asked.

"It was the two men from earlier."

"Atkar," sighed Warne

Leon looked at him. "Victor was here?"

"Yes. Like you, he wanted some stuff."

"What stuff did you give him?"

"I didn't. I put him off, hoping the authorities would pick him up before the handover. He is supposed to be locked up and out of our hair, for fuck sake."

That was it then. Atkar was out, and the old man wanted him found and quickly. So quickly that he was prepared to use an outlawed AID to find him. Leon thought.

* * *

Leon grabbed his phone and left the room as he called his father. His men stayed put, and Mr Warne was unusually quiet.

When Leon returned, he said to his men, "Bring him."

Leon's men grabbed Warne and took him out to the jetty. Warne saw no point in resisting or protesting. They bundled him into one of the fast inflatables, and the flotilla set off at speed downstream towards Teath docks. Warne knew the destination. The basement of the Kraxler Building. He hoped that it would not be his final destination.

34

For the rest of the day, Victor played with the things from Warne's container.

"How you get into that?" Posnanski asked, but the question sounded as though he already knew the answer. Or maybe it was just the effect of his accent.

Victor held the MFB in his hand. It resembled a shiny metallic hen's egg, but when activated, it looked more like a phone.

"I think it might be mine anyway," said Victor.

He squeezed the egg between the thumb and forefinger of his right hand. There was a slight vibration, and the surface changed from metallic to black. It flattened out, and one side became illuminated.

"Mine," said Victor with a smile.

"How—"

"It remembers the fingerprints and DNA of any of its previous owners. Can you sail this boat at night?"

"Can sail, but upriver difficult."

"It's getting dark. Can you get me back to the city? I can pay you now. I can move money to you using this." Victor lifted the MFB.

"Debt payment not just about money. Maybe I invest

money in venture with new friend."

Victor smiled. "It may be a bad investment."

"I only risk what I not have."

"True, I suppose. So, can you get us both back to the city?"

"Can sail to Teath docks. River wide. No engine, so wide river best."

"Into the lion's den!"

"What?"

"Never mind. Can you sail with no lights?"

"Yes."

"Okay. Get us to West Teath Docks. Not East. East would be bad."

"We leave once it full dark."

Victor was pleased that he had managed to make some of the fancy technology do his bidding as darkness fell. The MFB was now helping to guide Posnanski towards the mouth of the Tangreco River.

"Do you need me, or shall I try to sleep?" Victor asked.

"No. You sleep. It take three hours. Wind now help. Last time I sleep, boat attacked!" Posnanski smiled.

"Sorry," Victor said.

"I get sails up. You get anchor up."

By the time Victor had hauled the anchor, the sails were up, and the boat slipped south towards the mouth of the Tangreco River, leaving the desolate White islands glowing slightly in the blackness of the night. Victor left Posnanski on the helm, and he went below to get his head down. Sleep came fitfully as he tried to work out his next move. He needed quick transport around the city. The Silver Ghost was slow and limited. He had many contacts in the city, some shadier than others. Some very loyal to their Kraxler paymaster, all more loyal to themselves.

He settled on his move, and an exhausted sleep descended.

* * *

Just over three hours later, Posnanski woke Victor. "We at river mouth."

"Great." Victor sprang up, refreshed and instantly alert. He climbed on deck,

"We are on the East side of the river! We need to be on the other side."

"We will be, fifteen minutes," said Posnanski.

Victor looked at the East Bank skyline. Towering above all the other buildings was the Kraxler Building, with its lights on every floor shining out.

"Get us across. This is dangerous here. Kraxler will have boats patrolling the docks on this side. If they are looking for the Silver Ghost, we won't be able to outrun them."

"Boat going as fast as can to West. We have good speed."

Victor scanned the water and the dockside for movement. He could only hear the gentle hum of the breathing city and the creaking of the old wooden boat beneath him.

They were almost in mid-channel now. "Still clear?"

"I think so," said Victor. "Wait. I can hear an outboard! I can't see anything, but yes, I can definitely hear it. Getting closer, too."

"Get below. We play dead." Posnanski grabbed a rope from nowhere. He lashed the tiller to port and starboard quarters, locking their course in place. Both men went below deck. No lights. They closed the hatches.

"You still have the cargo net from yesterday?"

Posnanski grinned. "Useful," he said.

They prepared the cargo net and laid it at the foot of the companionway. They could both hear the approaching engine. Posnanski went to the fore cabin, lit a small oil lamp, and then closed the cabin door. They took up positions on either side of the companionway, holding the sides of the net, and waited.

"They go to the light when they come down," said Posnanski. "Then we have them."

They heard the inflatable come alongside and the muffled voices of its crew.

They heard footsteps above them on deck.

They heard the companionway hatch open.

They had seen no lights, and no light came down from above as the intruder descended with confidence. It was evident that he could see where he was going well enough.

Night vision tech! Victor thought.

He let go of the net and silently moved to the electrics panel he had discovered earlier. He nodded at Posnanski. Both men closed their eyes, and Victor threw a switch. The cabin lights flared to life. He turned them off again an instant later. He grabbed the net, and Posnanski wrapped the dazzled intruder in it. Posnanski grabbed the automatic gun, and Victor grabbed the night vision goggles.

An oily rag found its way into the intruder's mouth and the gun to his temple. Victor put a finger to his lips to indicate silence. The message was received.

Again, they waited.

A second man called down, "Anything?"

Getting no response, he started down but stopped and turned.

The intruder's footsteps could still be heard on the deck. Then they smelled it. The engine fuel being poured onto the deck was dripping through the gaps in the planking.

Victor and Posnanski looked at each other in the darkness but exchanged no words. Victor cut his captive free, and Posnanski kept the gun to his head.

"Up, and up quickly," whispered Victor.

The moment his head got to deck level, the shots rang out. The intruder's head swung backwards, and his body fell back between the other two men. There was not much face left to look at.

Both men remained silent. They had yet to show their presence. Maybe the gunman had been a bit trigger-happy, killing his colleague, mistakenly thinking him an enemy.

They heard footsteps on deck again.

They heard the inflatable engine start up.

They heard a whoosh and then a roar.

They heard the inflatable rush away.

Liquid fire began dropping through the decking planks.

35

There was no escaping it. The boat was doomed. The deck planking was ablaze, and Victor and Posnanski were trapped beneath it. The hatch was also ablaze.

"Put out fire when comes down," said Posnanski. His face was more sad than angry or frightened. "I get blankets. We cover us, and we get up and off."

Victor used cushions to smother the liquid fires as they dripped through the deck. The cabin was filling with smoke. Posnanski grabbed bedding from his cabin.

"Do you have any water down here to wet them?" Coughed Victor.

"Some. I get."

Posnanski found plastic bottles filled with water and threw a couple at Victor.

"Wet hair. Wet face. I wet bed."

Despite their predicament, Victor couldn't resist. "You don't look the type."

Posnanski looked at him without humour. "We must get off," he said

Victor thought the advice was a little unnecessary. Both men started wetting what would hopefully protect them as they tried to escape the flames.

"Cover hands!" said Victor

"Yes. Obv—" Posnanski failed to complete the sentence.

Both men were thrown forward through the main cabin, losing their footing and coming to rest on the cabin floor. The sound of wood splintering filled the cabin, followed by the sound of the water and the river.

"We hit something big," Posnanski said.

Victor looked towards the front of the boat. Water was running in through a hole big enough for a man to get through, but the force of the water entering made such an escape route impossible.

"Help move ballast," Posnanski ripped up the boards covering the bilges. The Keel was full of lead and scrap metal. Frantically, they hoisted lumps of it towards the stern of the boat. "Faster," he exclaimed.

Both men, working out like crazy, shifing most of the ballast to the back of the boat. There was no concern about damage. This was about survival. The water that had come in through the hole in the bow now made its way to the stern. The front end lifted out of the water enough to prevent water from coming in. The stern was perilously close to being overwhelmed by the river water, but at least the flames there had been quenched. They both managed to get to their feet and headed forward towards the hole in the bow.

Victor grabbed the items lifted from Warne's container, quickly fashioning a swag bag and throwing it over his shoulder.

Posnanski clambered through the hole, the waters of the Tangreco River lapping at him as he did so. He reached up and grabbed at the netting dangling, loosely now, from the bowsprit. With an effort, he managed to pull himself up and onto the bowsprit itself.

The front of the boat was lifting more and more now as the stern dipped below the waves. "Follow. Hurry. End soon comes." Posnanski shouted to Victor.

Posnanski rushed up the incline of the bowsprit and swung around the stay cable that was holding the now-burning headsail.

Victor was out now, too. "I can't get up holding this stuff!"

Posnanski was suddenly in mid-air, jumping for the quayside. He made it easily and shouted to Victor, "Throw it to me!"

Victor had no time to think about it. As the stern of the boat submitted to the river, he threw the swag bag straight into Posnanski's arms. Victor held on to the bowsprit netting, but the climb was becoming steeper and steeper, further away from the quayside.

"Quick!" Posnanski yelled.

Victor knew that he couldn't make it. He released his grip on the netting and fell back towards the hole just as a gust of wind blew the burning sail to where he had been struggling a moment before. He managed to keep most of his body outside the hole in the hull, but his left leg snagged on its edge, leaving a gash along his inner thigh. Victor shouted something at the boat and the waves. He struggled free and jumped into the water.

Posnanski had found a length of rope on the quayside. He threw the lifeline towards Victor and pulled him along the quayside to some granite steps. Victor climbed them on all fours before collapsing on the quayside.

Posnanski cast his eyes over his doomed boat. One half being consumed by fire and the other by the waters of the Tangreco River. Victor looked up at him and noticed the tears in his eyes. It might have been the smoke to blame, but the cause was more likely to be his boat slipping beneath the waves.

"I am so sorry, but your boat is gone," Victor said as he got to his feet.

"They will pay!" said Posnanski.

"They will all pay!"

Both men stood and silently watched the fire and water consume the Silver Ghost. The swag bag was at their feet. Once the boat was beneath the waters of the Tangreco River, they turned to each other. Neither spoke, but both understood.

The burning boat had drawn a crowd. The last thing Victor needed was a crowd. "Come on. We have to leave here," he said.

"Where we go?"

"Anywhere!"

They headed into Teath and away from the river. Victor looked up. Ahead of him, he could see Vantuba Prison over the top of the city buildings. It felt like he had been out of the place for weeks.

"Follow me," Victor said. "I have an old friend near here."

"Not Cody Warne, friend?"

"No. A proper friend."

Twenty minutes later, the two men stood outside the back door of a seedy nightclub called the Orange Room. After their recent travails, they could easily have fitted in with the garbage cans around the rear entrance.

Victor knocked on the door. There was silence. He tried again and lifted his eyes to see CCTV cameras looking down at him.

"Look up and smile," he said to Posnanski. He did so.

Victor knocked again without looking away from the camera. In a few seconds, the door opened.

A single female figure stood in the doorway—no muscle for protection, which was unusual in such places.

"Vic?" she said

"Athena. Please, can we come inside?"

"I thought you were inside."

"Well, not any more. Being inside here would help a lot, though."

"Get your sorry asses in here." She grabbed their arms and pulled them inside.

The club smelled like all drinking establishments when not in use. Stale drink and poorly maintained toilet facilities. Actually, they smelled like that all the time, but it was less noticeable when the people were drunk.

"Who is your friend, Vic?" said Athena.

"Who your friend Vic?" said Posnanski.

"Shall we have a quick drink? Then I will do the introductions." Victor said.

"The usual Vic?"

For a moment, he had to think what his usual was. It had been a long time since he had last had his usual.

"Please," he said, "Ice and no water."

"I know that!" She handed Victor the aniseed drink.

He sniffed it, sipped it, and then decided to wait for some ice to melt.

"And your unnamed friend?"

"Beer. Please."

She poured Posnanski a cloudy beer, added a slice of lemon, and handed it over. Then, she poured herself a clear spirit—no ice, no mixer.

"Shall we sit?" she indicated a booth slightly away from the bar. The men led the way and took their seats.

"This is Posnanski," said Victor. "He probably has a shorter one, but I don't know what it is. And this is the lovely Athena."

"So, do you have a shorter name?" she said

"Miklos."

"Miklos Posnanski?"

"It mean Victory People."

"Which?"

"Miklos. Posnanski mean get to know you."

"Please, can I call you Miklos? It's so much easier."

"Yes. And call you Vic?" Miklos said to Victor.

"And you can call me Athena til we know each other better."

They all nodded, raised their glasses to one another and drank.

"I need your help, A." said Victor.

"Seriously, I thought you were locked up. For kidnapping or killing your boss's daughter."

"I got out. I am not going back. I am already being hunted. Met Miklos along the way."

"You guys hungry?" Athena asked.

Both men just smiled.

A grubby-looking man appeared as if from nowhere. He had probably flowed along the sticky carpet as an oil slick would have done.

"Mason. Bring some of our hot food over from the kitchen. These friends of mine are cold and hungry. They will be staying for a while. Give them whatever they want. Treat them as V.I.P.s."

Mason carried just the hint of a stoop. He gave them all a thumbs-up.

Over the food, they discussed everything that had happened since the storm.

"Why are you two men apparently such good friends? You only just failed to kill each other," Athena said.

Victor gently shook his head, and Miklos shrugged. There was no answer.

Once they had eaten, Victor asked, "Do you have a couple of rooms upstairs and some clean clothes for us?"

"Follow me," she said. Oh, by the way, what's in the bag?"

"It's just some stuff I borrowed from someone. You still any good with a needle?"

Victor showed the still oozing wound in his arm where he had removed the locator beacon and his wounded inner thigh.

"Clean up first. Then I'll sort it," she said.

They went upstairs, and Athena showed them into two pokey little rooms, each with a bed and washing facilities.

"It's not palatial, but it will probably do for the night."

"Thanks, A. It will do perfectly."

Both men headed into their separate rooms.

Showered and dressed in a towel, Victor lay back on the bed. The food, drink and hot water had relaxed him. He dozed off.

"Mason, look after the club for a bit, would you? I might be a while."

Athena, med kit in hand, didn't knock. She found Victor asleep on the bed. She locked the door and went over to him. Gently, she put her hand on his chest and stroked him. Just as gently, he awoke. "Let's fix the arm," she said softly.

He held it out in front of her. She cleaned it and expertly stitched it in less than five minutes. Victor had not moved from the bed. "Thank you. It shows that you have done that before."

"I've done lots of things before," she said. Her hand dropped to his towel and gently tugged it open.

36

Sienna looked good in Carlos's clothes, but she didn't care anyway. She was just glad to be out of her apartment and out of the dead guard's clothes. The shower had taken ages. She managed to wash away the blood, but however hard she scrubbed, she couldn't wash away the deed.

"Do you know where Victor is?" Sienna asked Carlos

"Vantuba Prison."

"He was in Vantuba Prison. I think he just got out. Just escaped. Maybe just alive!"

Carlos reacted with a stunned silence, and before he could speak, Sienna cut in.

"I think I killed someone, Carlos. Well, I know I did!"

"What do you mean—"

"I fucking killed someone! One of the men guarding me. I didn't mean to. He was always nice to me. I hit him in the face with a bottle. I knocked him out and then accidentally smashed the back of his head on the floor. I killed him. Oh, Carlos, what am I going to do?"

"Slow down. Slow down."

"Can we go and find Victor? And—"

"Slow down and calm down. We must be careful here, or we will both end up in Vantuba prison with Victor."

"Well, what are we going to do? What if they find me? What if—"

"Slow down and calm down! Let me think."

Carlos headed for the drinks cabinet and poured two shots of a clear spirit.

"Here. One each."

He sat down, but Sienna remained standing in front of him, both deep in thought.

Neither drink touched the sides.

"Okay," he said. "Here's what we do—bloody clothes in black sacks. We will have to use my car to start with, but we need to get away from the house. Whoever had you locked away had a reason, and they probably knew about Victor. Which means they probably know about me."

Carlos threw whatever was easily portable from his refrigerator and wardrobe into a holdall. "Come on. We need to go!"

Sienna ran to the kitchen. "Scissors?"

"What? - Over there. Top drawer."

Sienna took the scissors in her right hand and a bunch of her long red hair in the other.

"Not here," said Carlos. "No point in easily confirming to anyone that you've been here. Do it in the car while I drive."

"Where are we going?"

"Anywhere."

"We need to find Victor. We need to get hold of my parents. We need to—"

"Be anywhere other than here."

Sienna gave in, and she followed Carlos to his car. She slumped into the passenger seat. Her mind and body spent. Carlos drove them away.

37

Sienna's body craved sleep and tried its very best to achieve it in the front of the car. Her mind was still racing, though.

"Carlos, I know who imprisoned me."

"What!"

"I know who it was. It was my father." Sienna almost whispered it.

Carlos stopped the car. He looked straight forward through the windscreen. Processing.

Eventually, the cogs stopped, and he turned to Sienna.

"Why? Why would he do that?"

"I saw him kill Sam."

Carlos resumed his inspection of the windscreen, and the cogs turned again.

"He didn't know what to do with you. Anyone else would not be alive to talk about this. The old bastard locked you up while he decided what to do. And he tried to blame Victor for everything. We can't let him find you. We have to find Victor."

More windscreen inspection, then Carlos pulled out.

"Where are we going?" Sienna asked.

"Not sure. Still thinking."

"I need to find Victor."

How do you know he's out?'

Sienna explained how she had manipulated the news feed with the software and seen Victor jump from the cliff top. She described her own escape and the inadvertent demise of one of her guards.

"Where would he go?" Sienna demanded.

"We need to get you somewhere safe and find Victor."

Sienna emitted an exhausted, "Where?"

"Your mother? Your grandmother?"

"No. We need to go somewhere not controlled by my father."

"I don't think he controls Isabella, but he could look for us there," Carlos said.

"So, where?"

"I know a place. I know a place where he wouldn't think of looking for you. You should be safe for a while. Then we can concentrate on finding Victor."

"So, where?"

"You won't fit in, but it won't matter."

Sienna gave in to the fatigue, stopped talking, and closed her eyes.

Carlos turned the car down a left turn and off the main thoroughfare. Twenty minutes later, he pulled up on the riverside in Maybyn.

Carlos gently shook Sienna awake. "Come on. Follow me."

They abandoned the car and headed along the river on foot. Five minutes later, they stood outside a bar that seemed to cater for more than just food and drink. The signage above the door, intended to indicate ownership, conveyed the customer message perfectly.

"Fanny's and Dick's."

38

"Fanny and Dick?" Sienna said.

"No. Fanny's and Dick's," Carlos replied.

"So more than one fanny and more than one dick?"

"The sign is old and deliberately misleading. If you look closely, very closely, you can see apostrophes."

"Oh. So owned by Fanny and Dick?"

"Exactly," Carlos confirmed. "Come on. Let's get inside, off the street, then you'll get it."

Sienna followed Carlos into the seedy establishment. Once inside the door, they could smell the stale drink emanating from the floorboards and the smoke. Smoke that could get you high.

They headed for the bar.

"What… What is this place?" Sienna said.

"Sienna! Look over there." Carlos pointed to the booths on the left side of the place. "Then look over there." Indicating the right side of the place.

"Close your mouth, Sienna. It looks undignified with you wandering around with it gaping."

"It's a gay bar…"

"Sharp Sienna, Sharp," Carlos said sarcastically.

Sienna was no longer gaping, but her mouth wasn't closed. It talked.

"Okay... all boys on that side and all girls on that side. Where shall we sit?"

"The etiquette is for any mixed couples to stand at the bar. Be warned, though. Some of the girls might try to get you over there, and some of the boys might try to get me over here." Carlos indicated alternate sides of the bar.

"I don't fancy that, Carlos."

"Not really the time for such things, is it? Let's get a drink at the bar."

They wandered over to the bar, behind which was a young lad and a young lady.

"Two beers."

"No problem, Carlos," said the barman and Sienna raised an eyebrow.

"This place, as it's laid out, is not very conducive to us having a private chat, is it?" Sienna pointed out.

Carlos nodded and turned to the barman.

"Can we go upstairs for half an hour? Oh, and can you send up some hot food, too?" Carlos asked.

The barman looked strangely at the pair of them.

"Well, yes, you can, but is this the best place, Carlos? I mean, you two as a couple wanting a room in a gay bar is not exactly fitting in, is it?"

"Good," Carlos said. "Put the beers, food and the room on my account. And the usual privacy. Okay. You haven't seen us."

"The quicker you two get on with it, the better. To be honest, you aren't really good for our image." The barman handed Carlos a room key.

"Fuck off," Carlos said, but in a very friendly tone.

Sienna and Carlos made their way through a doorway just behind the bar and up a set of stairs to the first floor. Carlos let them into Room Four.

"It smells of sex in here," Sienna complained.

"Of course it does. And how do you know what sex smells like, Sienna?"

She didn't reply and didn't sit on the bed. She took a chair in the corner instead, under the impression that it might be less soiled than the bed. Carlos jumped on the bed and stretched out.

"Carlos!"

" I know. We need to get to Victor."

"Soon, Carlos."

"I know. Drink your beer and give me those scissors you picked up at my place. You need a trim."

Carlos did a half-decent job of cutting Sienna's long red locks. The locks fell to the floor, leaving her with a slightly masculine, ragged, short-haired arrangement.

"What do you think? I like it. You could pass for your sister now. Well, you could if you were blonde." Carlos said.

"I hate it," Sienna replied, but her face betrayed her real feelings about the dramatic change in style. She smiled at Carlos.

The knock at the door brought them back to reality. Carlos motioned for Sienna to hide behind the door, and he opened it slightly. The barman from downstairs held two large bowls of vegetable pasta, which he handed to Carlos.

Carlos nodded his thanks and shut the door. They both finished their meals and beer.

"Okay. Now Victor. You stay here, and I will go and make a call." Carlos said

"Where from? Can't you do it from here?" Sienna asked.

"Will do it from somewhere else in case it gets traced. Stay here until I get back."

"No. I will come with you. I need to speak to him."

"Sienna. I speak to him often. It won't seem suspicious if I call. If you call—"

"Okay. Be quick."

39

Carlos believed that Sienna believed that Victor had escaped. He wanted confirmation, though.

He didn't want to go too far, but he knew that any call could be monitored and traced. He headed out of Fanny's and Dick's onto the street. He turned left and headed towards Harvey's, another bar along the river. It was one he frequented, and it was dark inside. He went in and went up to the bar.

"Can I use your house phone, please?" Carlos asked.

"Why. Why can't you use your mobile?"

"It's important. You know what mobiles are like these days."

"Would you like a drink?"

Carlos could see that he needed to oil the wheels.

"Tell you what. I'll have a drink. You have a drink." Carlos suggested.

After a short silence, the bartender poured two beers and two shots of clear spirit.

Carlos put more than enough money on the bar to cover the tab. He picked up the beer and clinked glasses with the bartender.

They both drank. The tense atmosphere mellowed as the

beer disappeared.

Carlos reached for the shot, and his drinking partner put his hand over Carlos's to stop him.

"Only after you have made your call."

Carlos took the offered handset and headed to a quiet corner.

He punched in the memorised number of the Vantuba prison. He had used it often enough. It rang and rang. No answer. Carlos gave the phone back to the barman.

"No luck," Carlos said. "But thank you."

"Who were you after?"

"Just enquiring after someone in Vantuba prison. No one is answering ."

"Not surprised. There has been a fire there."

"What!"

"Yep. A fire. And maybe some escapees."

"How do you know this?"

"Sources."

"What sources?" Carlos put more money on the bar.

"Never mind my sources. They are reliable, though."

Carlos put more money on the table. "Who has escaped?"

"Let's drink."

Both men did so together, and then the barman disappeared out back with the phone and the money.

When he returned, he said, "I know who got out. Only one."

"Who?"

Silence.

"Look, I have no money left."

Silence.

"Okay. Thanks for the drinks and the phone." Carlos turned to leave.

"One of Kraxler's lot. Victor Atkar. How the mighty have fallen."

Carlos had stopped in his tracks. He turned back to the barman.

"Thank you. I will come back for a drink with you another day." Carlos smiled.

The barman smiled and nodded. Carlos headed quickly back to find Sienna.

40

Carlos almost ran through Fanny's and Dick's to the bar at the back. There were no bar staff to be seen. He went around the back and up the stairs. He knocked on the door of Room Four. No reply. He tried the door. It opened with a slight creak.

"Sienna?" He whispered.

He went on into the room—no sign of Sienna anywhere.

"Shit, shit, shit!" Carlos thought.

He went back into the corridor and shouted. "Sienna!"

After a moment or two, the bar staff from earlier came out of room six, closely followed by Sienna.

"What?" She exclaimed.

The lady bartender said, "So we are all fine now, yeah? This room don't smell of sex."

"For fuck sake, Sienna!" Carlos exclaimed.

Sienna had never before seen Carlos this angry. He manhandled her into the sweet-smelling Room Six and slammed the door shut behind himself as he followed her in. He ignored the disgruntled muttering from outside the door.

"Sit down, Sienna. I have some news for you."

"What?"

"You were right. Victor escaped during the storm."

"Well, where is he now?"

"I don't know Sienna. I don't know."

"Where would he go? Everyone will be looking for him. I need to see him, Carlos. I need to see him!"

"Come here and calm down. You need an Atkar hug. They are special, you know. They come from a love of the land and a love of people. They come from the love of friends and the love of family. Come here."

They hugged for many moments, and eventually, Carlos pulled away. They both had wet cheeks.

"That was beautiful what you said about Atkar hugs," Sienna said.

"Which bits?"

"Oh, I don't know. Love of the land and of family, of friends."

Carlos pulled away further. Arms length now.

"You are a genius, Sienna! I know where he is, or at least I know where he is going."

"Where?"

"Oakwood. Our home village. Our home village was destroyed. Our home village, where our parents were murdered."

Sienna considered it.

"But he might be dead, Carlos."

"If he is, then we can't help him. If he isn't, I am sure he will head for Oakwood. We have this room for the night. We will sleep first if we can. And we will think. We need to do the thinking thing, Sienna. Who are Victor's enemies, and who are his friends? Who are our enemies and who are our friends?"

"Carlos. Shut up and get into bed."

"I will sleep on the floor," Carlos said.

"Carlos. Get into bed with me. I need one of those Atkar hugs. Unless I have misjudged events today, I don't think I have anything to worry about sleeping in the same bed as you."

"You don't. And even if you had misunderstood some of the revelations of the day, you would still be fine. Atkar's are decent folk."

They both got into bed.

41

Kelvin was reasonably sure that Victor was dead. He was also reasonably confident that even if he were alive, he would be captured and re-incarcerated quickly. Reasonably sure, but not absolutely so.

His phone rang, and he accepted the call. It was his son, Leon, and he cut straight to the chase.

"Victor has just visited Cody at his compound," Leon said.

"Where is he now?"

"Don't know. He can't be far away. He has no way of getting around the city."

"Okay. Just bring in the hardware."

"Victor has it."

"What!"

"Victor has it."

Kelvin cut the call with no further instructions to his son.

Almost immediately, Kelvin's phone rang again, and he accepted the call from one of his most trusted people, hoping for some good news. He was just about to call him with the news of Atkar anyway.

"Floyd! You are calling with good news from the troops on

the ground searching for Atkar?" Kelvin said.

"Not exactly," Floyd replied in his rasping tones.

"Not exactly? What is it then?"

"The valuable package that we had in safekeeping whilst you decided what to do with it..." Floyd left the subject hanging.

"What?" Kelvin demanded, with more than a little impatience showing in his voice.

"The package is no longer in our care. It looks like it caused one fatality when it left our care."

Kelvin carefully reversed into a chair, saying nothing into the phone. At last, he regained the power of speech, but the returning voice had a distinct tremor now.

"Find the package at all costs, Floyd! Do it very quickly. I cannot countenance any... what shall we call it... leakage from the package. And also remember that the package is delicate and is not to be harmed."

"So delicate that a man is dead at her hand."

"Floyd. Do I have to spell it out? Sort it out with efficiency and discretion, which is what I pay you for. Move some resources from finding Atkar. We may even find him with the package. They have a history."

"I take it that there is no need to treat Atkar with the same delicacy as the package."

"No. Check out Atkar's brother, too. Sort it."

Floyd disconnected the call.

Kelvin couldn't believe it: Victor had escaped a high-security prison, and Sienna had escaped his clutches—on the same day!

42

The inflatables tore down the river, their outboards' noise advertising the fact that expensive and hard-to-come-by fuel was no problem for the Kraxler organisation. Cody was in the lead boat, and he was not comfortable. His hands were tied behind his back, and his feet were tied together, too. The ride downriver had been fast and wet, with spray coming over the bow on each bounce. Unable to steady himself, Warne slipped from his seat into the floor of the boat, joining the salty river water. It, and he, now smelled of outboard fuel. He was just able to keep his face out of the water. None of his captors showed any concern. Leon liked driving the boat, and he liked driving it fast. He liked driving it from a standing position as it gave him more stability. Passenger comfort was not at the top of his list, and even the properly seated were being bounced around. Warne's bouncing was markedly less comfortable than that of the other passengers. His tattooed face was softened up and bruised as the boats slowed to approach the Kraxler building.

The Kraxler building was situated right on the riverfront, and Leon guided the inflatables under a rectangular concrete arch, taking them away from the prying eyes of the city. The boats were secured to a wooden pontoon, and Leon, a big and powerful man, lifted the slight Cody Warne from the boat's hull to his feet. He then, none too gently, helped him onto the pontoon. Neither man nor any of the entourage spoke while Warne's feet were freed and he was manoeuvred along the pontoon and into the depths of the Kraxler building proper.

The group travelled down several flights of stairs and into a large square room that looked like builders might return at any moment to resume work. Tools and building materials were everywhere, and the room was windowless, being below river level.

Finally, Leon spoke to Warne. "Stay here."

Leon and his men left through a doorway at the rear of the room. There was, however, no door to close—more evidence of shabby building work. Warne remained standing and bound. His captors having left, he decided to have a look around the room, but he had no intention of leaving. There would be a business transaction later, he was sure. He just wasn't sure that he would benefit from it. But he might.

43

The Orange Room Club was busy. Mason was still in charge while Athena was upstairs, and he was pretty sure that the current state of affairs would continue until at least the early hours of the morning. He knew Victor's face from his previous visits.

Opportunities, opportunities. Mason thought.

He quietly went to the back office and sat in Athena's swivel chair behind her desk. He felt confident that she was too busy upstairs with Victor Atkar to be catching him in the forbidden confines of her office. He picked up the only phone in the club and punched in a number. There was no reply from Cody Warne.

He knew that going further up the food chain would be more difficult, more risky, but potentially much more rewarding. As he pondered, he riffled through Athena's desk and found a number that might be of use. His hands were trembling now. Should he make the call?

He punched in the number and waited for the connection. It took a while, but eventually, the other end picked up as he nervously swivelled in the chair.

"Who is this?"

Mason would not give his name. "Do you know that Victor

Atkar is out?"

"How do you know?"

"I have seen him, and I know where he is."

"Where?"

"From the tone of your voice, it seems this is important to you."

"Where is he?"

"We can trade? I give you the information, and you reward me." Mason was in bargaining mode.

"I can trace this number in minutes. And be there before you have time to take a shit."

"I didn't say I was with, or near, Atkar."

"True. But you would become one more person on my list of people I need to find. And I will find Atkar, and I will find you."

Mason was losing his nerve rapidly. "Uh, Okay."

"Okay, what?"

"Okay, I will tell you where he is, but some gratitude or future favour would be good."

"You will get what you deserve. Let me have your name so that I can organise it."

"Mason Goldsmith. I work at the Orange Room Club. Atkar is upstairs."

The call was terminated, and Mason Goldsmith found himself no longer engaged in conversation or negotiation. He swung the chair around as he replaced the phone on the desk where he had found it.

Smiling to himself, he softly said, "I will get my reward. Back to work in this shit hole for now, though."

44

Athena's hand dropped to Victor's towel and gently tugged it open.

Victor could not hide his body's automatic response to the touch of an attractive woman, especially given how long it had been since it had last happened. His hand gently fell onto hers, and he firmly stopped its southward progress.

"Sorry, A. I know you've done lots of things. We have done lots of things. But I can't do this with you now." Victor's mind and body were obviously in total disagreement on the subject.

"Victor?" Athena questioned as she looked him in the eye.

"Oh," Athena said.

"Yes. Oh."

"There is someone else more important to you than this?" Her eyes moved again to just below his waist.

"More important. Yes. Sorry."

"One day, our stars will align, Victor Atkar. When that happens…. Well, when that happens, we will both know about it!"

"One day." Victor issued the consolation with a smile.

Athena got up from the bed and headed for the door.

"Get some sleep. If you can sleep with that." Again, her

eyes were fixed just below Victor's waist.

"Thanks, A. You are one of those stars that might align."

She closed the door behind her and headed back to work.

45

Mason looked up from the replaced phone and toward the office door as he emerged from Athena's chair. He looked straight into the eyes of the chair's owner, who was standing in the doorway.

Athena Ambrose was not quick to temper. She had learned over the years that taking a couple of breaths improved the consideration of the matter at hand. She had taken more than a couple of breaths whilst listening to Mason on the phone. As with most people not quick to temper, the temper, once established, was both severe, long-lasting and sometimes scarily quiet.

"Athena!" Mason exclaimed.

Athena said nothing and was motionless in the doorway.

"I…I…" Mason stammered.

"Who?" She almost whispered.

"Who?"

"Who were you talking with? No bullshit, and make it quick, and you might, possibly, make it out of this room." Athena again spoke so quietly that Mason could hardly hear her.

Mason stood as a man who was defeated and as a man who did not know what to do.

"It was…"

"Now! Tell me now!" Athena's temper had reached the surface despite her best efforts. It was not a pretty sight for Mason.

She took a step into the room. Both its occupants were visibly shaking.

"Now!" She said quietly, but with an unmistakable menace in her tone.

After a pause, Mason said, "Leon Kraxler."

It was Athena's turn to pause. Then she said to Mason, "You get to leave the room after all. Come with me, and we will sort out your stupid, greedy mess."

Relieved at her response, Mason moved from behind Athena's desk, briefly considered speaking, but silently followed towards the door.

Mason did not possess the coordination to mix cocktails in the bar. This same fundamental feature caused him to fail to evade Athena's foot, connecting with his tenderest bodily parts as she turned to face him in the corridor.

He buckled over and cried out through a grimace.

Athena's coordination again exceeded Mason's, as her other foot connected with his descending head. She caught him before he hit the floor.

"Right. Back into my chair, I think." She guided the stunned and terrified Mason back behind her desk and dumped him in the chair. She turned away from him to the cabinet against the wall. She grabbed a roll of tape and used it to attach all four of Mason's limbs to the chair. He would not be moving without help. She picked up the phone and pressed the redial button. Without waiting for it to connect, she forced it into Mason's mouth and taped it there.

She left the office and, on this rare occasion, locked the door behind her.

* * *

Athena raced up the stairs to Victor's room. She didn't knock. She strode in and yelled at Victor, "Victor. We have to leave! Now! Come on! One useless bastard has betrayed you and fucked me over, too. I will lose this place now, and you will lose more than that unless we leave right now."

Victor was already gathering his stuff.

Athena said, "I need to get some things. We taking Miklos?"

"We?" Victor questioned.

"Yeah. We! Get Miklos if you want, but we need to be gone in five minutes minimum." Athena left the room at speed.

At a similar rate, Victor headed for Miklos's room. He didn't knock.

"Miklos! Hurry. We need to go. We are not safe here."

Miklos was lying on the bed.

"We go then."

Miklos grabbed his stuff, and they headed downstairs with Victor to join Athena.

46

Leon picked up the phone as he drove. It was the same number as the one from which the tip-off call had come. Weird, unintelligible sounds were all he could hear.

He turned briefly to his sidekick, "How long till we get to The Orange Room?"

"About ten minutes, give or take." The sidekick said.

"And we have three cars full of our crew." Leon thought out loud. No one answered.

"Anyone been to this club before? Does anyone know the layout?" Leon enquired.

From the back seat, one of the men replied, "It's a dive. Tables and chairs in the front. Think there are offices at the rear and rooms upstairs."

"Standard club layout, then. Thanks for the enormously helpful in-depth assessment of the place." Leon's sarcasm got lost somewhere between his driver's seat and the passengers in the back.

The convoy sped through the city, letting everyone en route know that powerful people were passing through. It rounded the last corner and stopped outside the front of The Orange Room.

Leon was the first out of the vehicles and headed straight

for and through the main entrance to the club. It wasn't busy. He could see no staff around, and he scouted the place out with a few sweeps of his gaze.

"Up here," Leon said, pointing at the stairs in the corner. "Come on. He is supposed to be upstairs."

Leon led the snake of men up to the landing. They had all drawn their weapons. When they reached the landing, Leon turned towards the first door and kicked it open. The room was empty. He backed out of the room and did the same thing to the next door, which was empty, too. All the rooms along the landing turned out to be empty.

Leon was furious. "We're too late! We've missed him. We can't have missed him by much. I'll stay here with the front car people and see what I can find. The rest of you take the other two cars and search the area. He can't be far away, and he's probably on foot."

His men did not seem to be too keen to leave the building. Leon showed his impatience. "Get on with it! We need to find him, and we need to find him quickly. Split up and search on foot. You lot go north of the club, and you lot south. We'll head towards the river when we've finished here. Meet back here in an hour. Hopefully, with Atkar, but if not, we will need to regroup."

Leon sat on the bed of the last room he entered at the far end of the corridor. He looked around the room. There was nothing obvious to see. There were no clues as to who had last been in these rooms. No clues as to whether Victor had even been here.

Upstairs was clear. There was no sign of Victor anywhere. Leon headed downstairs to check out all the rooms there. He wasn't confident that Victor would still be around, even if he had been here at all. But he had to check. Downstairs with his men, he started exploring the backrooms.

* * *

Leon kicked in the door to Athena's office. Mason was still in her chair, and he was still trying to eat the telephone. Leon went over to him and gently removed the device from his mouth.

"Where is Atkar?" Leon said

"Last time I saw him, he was upstairs," said Mason through a dry mouth.

"Did you see him leave? Was he alone? Quick answers would be appreciated!"

"Well, you haven't shown much appreciation so far."

"Do you know what the opposite of appreciation is?"

"Huh?"

"Thought not. The opposite of appreciation is depreciation. So, currently, your value to me is depreciating rapidly. You are taped to a chair and will not be receiving any reward from me. The river is not far away, and that chair would take you straight to the riverbed. Let's forget about rewards, shall we?"

"He was with my boss, Athena Ambrose. She owns this place. And he was with another guy with a foreign name. They have been quite tight over the last few hours. I didn't see them leave, though."

"Where would they have gone? Does this Ambrose woman have any other places close by?"

"She knows a lot of people in a lot of places. She could've gone anywhere. They could all have gone anywhere, together or apart. I don't know!"

Leon had had enough. He reinserted the phone, with vigour, into Mason's mouth.

"Call me when you know more," he said, and then he turned and left the room with his henchmen in tow.

"You checked all the other rooms out back?"Leon said.

"All except the kitchen," said one of the men.

"I'll do it, shall I?" Leon was in full sarcastic mode. His

men did not reply.

Leon found nothing in the kitchen except a pan full of oil on the stove. He lit the burner beneath it. Then, he returned to his men.

"Okay. Let's join the others on the search—busy night." Leon said.

47

John had chatted with some of his work friends. They had given him several opinions as to where he could get covert help in his quest to find Sienna. Some of the people he didn't want to get involved with. They were terrible, and he would never be free of them. Some would prove useless and probably expensive. He chose the middle road and decided to make any arrangements in person, so he could assess their credibility before proceeding.

He headed off to the Orange Room Club to find a lady called Athena Ambrose.

John walked his way to the club. It was a way for him to gather his thoughts. He had heard of the place but had never been to it. He could see the club along the street as he turned the corner. Outside, three black SUVs were parked.

Don't like the look of that.

He slowed his pace and eventually came to a stop. He sat himself down on a low wall across the road from the Orange Room Club.

Patience, John, patience. Black SUVs mean trouble. Wait until they have gone.

He lit up a smoke.

Before his smoke was finished, a group of men left the club and discussed matters on its doorstep. They split in two and headed off on foot, unenthusiastically, in opposite directions.

John concluded that the unmoved SUVs indicated unfinished business. He continued his smoke. Just as he stubbed out the butt, another group of men left the building. They also went to the SUVs, and they too did not drive off. They displayed much more urgency, though. Then they headed off in the direction of the river. John waited, unconvinced that whatever was happening here was over.

Give it ten minutes, just time for another smoke.

John added a second butt to the street and crossed to the pub entrance. The place was deserted. It seemed that men in SUVs were bad for business. He went on further into the club. Eventually, he made it to the back office and opened its door.

In front of him was a man taped to a swivel chair with a phone in his mouth. The man seems to be testing out the swivel function of the chair, and his eyes seem to plead with John.

The man in the chair had obviously pissed off the men from the SUVs, and John was not keen to find himself in a similar position. He needed to make some progress, though. He headed over to the man in the chair and extracted the phone.

“Looks like you've pissed off some nasty men,” John said.

“Well, you've got that one wrong, pal! Not men, just one woman."

"So what's with all the men leaving here a few minutes ago? They obviously paid you a visit. And they left you attached to the chair, so you must've pissed them off somewhat.”

"Well, I haven't pissed you off, so please, could you cut me free?"

"Why?”

“Why what"?

“Why should I cut you free?”

“Because I will be grateful. Come on. Cut me loose.”

“But I would then be pissing off whoever put you in that chair.”

“She’s gone. The men have gone. Cut me loose.”

“And your gratitude will outweigh me pissing off the woman and pissing off the men. So how grateful?"

“Well, that depends. Who are you? I've not seen you here before, so why are you here? What do you want?”

"Okay. I need some help to find someone. You help with that?"

"If I can’t, I can find someone who can,” Mason said.

“Who?”

“Cut me loose. I can help. Too many people are going missing today.”

“Too many people?”

“Yeah. Victor Atkar… missing. Whoever you are looking for… missing.”

“Victor Atkar is missing?”

“Well, my recent visitors can’t find him. Who are you looking for?”

John remained silent, deep in thought.

A “Whoosh” from the kitchen broke the silence. It wasn’t loud. A few moments later, crackling sounds made themselves heard in the office.

“What’s that?” Mason asked John.

“How should I know? I’m the visitor. It’s your place, no?”

“Shit! I can smell smoke. It’s fire! Cut me loose. Please!”

John turned and left the office, scouting out the kitchen pyrotechnics before returning to the unsettled Mason in the swivel chair.

“Yep! It’s a fire. You leave a chip pan on the stove?”

"Cut me loose!"

John returned to the kitchen and hunted in some of the drawers. Through the smoke, he found a knife and headed back to Mason. Mason was now in full panic mode, trying to manoeuvre himself and the swivel chair through a gap between the desk and the wall. The gap was too small, and Mason was not the most agile.

"Please, please, please cut me loose."

"Will you help me find my missing person?"

"Yes! Yes!"

The office was filling with black smoke, which only increased the panic of the man in the chair.

"Okay. Deal." John said.

John went behind the desk and began cutting the tape that confined the struggling and agitated Mason to the chair.

"It will be quicker if you keep still," explained John.

Mason struggled with the instructions but obeyed, and eventually, John set him free. Mason ran for the street. John snatched the phone from the desk and followed him out.

John reached the door and found Mason doubled over, looking at the ground, gasping for air and rubbing his wrists. John spotted a group of men heading down the street towards them. They didn't seem to be in a hurry.

John grabbed Mason under one of his arms and lifted him up.

"Come on. Your friends are nearly back. We need to go."

Mason immediately stopped his theatrical display and accompanied John down the street, away from the approaching SUV men.

48

Victor, Miklos and Athena had heard the SUVs pull up at the front of the Orange Room.

"Come on. There is always a rear entrance," Athena pointed out.

"Well, let's use it as an exit, shall we?" Victor said.

Miklos nodded. All three of them headed out the back way into the street.

"They haven't even thought of covering the back. Dim!" Athena said.

"Not yet," Miklos chipped in.

"Come on—enough chat. Let's get out of here. Let's head for the river to start with." Victor suggested.

They headed east, towards the river. Athena knew the immediate vicinity very well, and they soon found themselves well away from the club.

"We need to slow down," Athena said, panting. "Running means running.... To something or from something. And three people doing it together is bound to draw attention."

They slowed to a more sedate pace and made it to the river. Victor stopped, and the other two did so a couple of paces later, and they turned to face Victor.

"Now what?" Miklos said.

"Now we split up. You two have already put yourselves in harm's way for me. We split up." Victor said.

"We together till I paid," Miklos said. There was something in his facial expression that overcame the barriers of verbal communication.

They were in this together now.

Athena gazed off into the distance over Victor's head. She said nothing, but her features changed.

Victor turned and looked behind himself. "What is it?"

"That glow. That glow is coming from the Orange Room! That orange glow *is* the Orange Room!" Athena's voice trailed off.

"Who?" Miklos asked.

"That traitorous bastard that I gave a job to. Mason Goldsmith. He gave you up, Victor. He gave you up to Leon Kraxler. And when he didn't find you there, Kraxler must have torched the club."

"Why would Leon Kraxler want me recaptured so badly? Why would any of the Kraxlers want me recaptured so badly?"

Athena had an edge to her voice now that cut through the air.

"Wake up, Victor! They don't want to recapture you. They want you dead. Can't you remember your trial? They worked very hard in the background for the death penalty. You only just got away with a life sentence."

"But I was their friend. They treated me like family. I treated them like family."

"And your time in Vantuba prison… time to think about that. And nothing! Nothing popped into your head during that time as to why the all-powerful Kraxlers have turned against you?"

Victor looked and felt like a wounded man. He went over to the fence by the river and supported himself on it.

"Still nothing popping into your thick head? It must be something bad."

"Sienna. It must be about Sienna. But they all know that I wouldn't hurt her, that I would not have abducted her, that I haven't harmed her in any way. All the family would know that. She was like a sister to me."

"Well, Sienna would be up there enough on the scale of things to cause all this grief."

"They know I wouldn't. They know I didn't. They know…"

Victor's voice trailed off and then, after a pause, came back strong.

"They know!"

"Know what?" Athena asked.

After another pause, Victor came back again.

"They know. They know that I was seeing Sienna."

Silence hit the trio, eventually broken again by Victor.

"That's it. That's what it is. That's what all this is about. It makes sense. It makes sense, except for Sienna's disappearance. So where is Sienna? What happened to her?"

Athena broke the silence, "Wanting you dead is a bit harsh for seeing your sister. Well, kind of stepsister. Well, a kind of family friend, like a sister. And they did want, do want, you dead."

"Exactly! She is not my sister. She was like my sister. All five of us as kids were like a family. The Kraxler house and the Keogh house were next door to each other, but they might as well have been one big place. Adults and children just came and went in each house."

Miklos was getting bored with this. "We need go."

49

Connie's farm was in a quiet valley that could only be accessed on foot. Not many people bothered, so she had a peaceful time. Her animals were kept in enclosures and pretty much fended for themselves while she was away from the farm. She did this often, trekking into the peaks and camping under the stars. She loved the mountains. The more she was in the mountains, the more she loved them. She loved the open spaces and the fresh air. She loved the bird song and the sounds of flowing fresh water. She loved the animals that she kept on her farm. She also loved being away from the majority of her family.

She was away from the farm now. Alone. Connie's tent was only a few meters from the lakeshore. She awoke and clambered out, naked, into the sunny morning. Dew still lay on the grass and wet the palms of her hands and her knees. She stood up, stretched, and headed down towards the lake. She waded in until she was thigh-deep and then plunged headfirst into the lake's cold waters. She surfaced and gasped as the cold water took her breath away. Ten minutes of gentle swimming on her back, and she was done. Fully refreshed and just starting to feel a little hungry, she exited the lake. The quickly warming sun dried her as she sat on a rock. She had made a campfire next to the tent the previous evening, but it had died overnight. She still had some spare foraged fuel, so she rebuilt and relit the fire. Coffee first.

She felt her hunger increase as she cooked her breakfast. She also craved contact with her grandmother, whom she hadn't spoken to for a couple of weeks. Only Isabella had kept in regular contact, and even that had not been in person. Messages were passed along to family and friends via Isabella, as were the replies.

Connie ducked into the tent to grab one of the bits of illegal tech she had lifted from the Kraxler building on her last day in the city. Tech was deemed illegal if it was above a certain level of sophistication. Regular phones were nicely placed in a grey area. The authorities, or what remained of them these days, liked to play games in such grey areas. The tech Connie was using was not in a grey area. It was fully illegal, but no one would challenge her use of it. She was a Kraxler.

She hit the button on the front and waited. Her grandmother answered quickly.

"Connie! How are you?" Isabella said

"I'm all good. Just had a skinny dip in the lake, coffee, and now cooking up some breakfast. I'll pack up the tent later and head back to the farm for a few days. Any news from back home in the big bad city? Still no news of Sienna, I suppose?"

"No. No news of Sienna. But there is some news about Victor."

"I don't think I want to know."

"Yes, I think you would want to know. It appears that he has escaped from Vantuba Prison. Your lovely father seems to have got the whole city on high alert to recapture him," Isabella said.

"I know we've talked about it before, but I really don't

think Victor had anything to do with Sienna's disappearance, or Sam's. He wasn't around on the day it all went pear-shaped. And he loved Sam. She was another mother for him." Connie said.

"Has anyone from the city been out to see you at the farm or in the mountains?"

"No, Iz. I think the city has mostly forgotten about me. Grandmothers excepted, of course." Connie said.

"When are you going to come back?"

"You know the answer to that. I'll come back when Sienna tells me to. Iz, I can still remember her face. I can still remember the look on it. There was a fear in her eyes. A fear for herself and a fear for me. It was a look of fear and total incomprehension."

"But what happens if we never hear from her again? Will you stay in the mountains forever?"

Connie carried on as if she hadn't heard her grandmother.

"Father must know something. I don't even know if he was there that day."

Then she returned to the previous topic: "We will hear from her again. I'm convinced of it. She is somewhere around. She just can't get to us at the moment."

"Connie…"

"It will be fine."

"Just be careful when you go back to the farm. Keep a lookout for any strangeness."

"I will. It will be fine," deflecting, she followed on with, "How's mum? How is your fleet of sailing boats?"

"Your mum is fine, considering she is effectively down two daughters; her only son seems to be following in his father's footsteps, and her best friend is still missing, too."

Connie sensed the danger in continuing with that conversation. "And your boats?"

Isabella warmed to the new topic. "They are making me

money now. Now that we have trained up some decent manpower to sail the things. Sailing was a bit of a lost art. Fuel is so expensive now. The wind is free if you have the right people."

Connie's breakfast was now past being ready.

"That's excellent. My breakfast is burning. Got to run. Love to all in the big city."

With a note of sadness, Isabella said, "Bye, Connie. Love back."

Connie cut the call and tucked into her fried breakfast.

Time to check in on the farm. Dress, pack up and head down the valley.

50

"She was like a sister but not a sister," Victor repeated more quietly.

Quietly enough to allow the rapidly approaching motor vehicles to be heard.

"Shit," Athena said.

"Quick. Follow." Miklos said.

They obeyed, and Miklos guided them down to a rickety wooden pontoon at the water's edge. Tied up at one end was a decent-sized old wooden rowing punt. Handy oars signified both recent use and little local theft.

"Get in. Cover. I row. Careful old nails."

There was no time for discussion. Victor and Athena lay in the bottom of the wooden punt, covering themselves with the tarp that had filled the bow section.

"Literally… bloody nails everywhere!" Victor complained from beneath the tarp.

Miklos untied the boat and gently pushed off. He sat on the bench seat across the middle of the boat and started, very gently, to row into the middle of the channel. He was facing the shore, so he could see the black SUVs arrive at the roadside on the bank. He saw the men get out.

"Men here." Miklos quietly addressed the covered

occupants of the punt.

"They only look Victor. They not look me. They not look Athena."

On the shore, Leon looked around and instructed his men to search the area. He called out to the punt.

"You. Where are you going? Come back here."

Miklos replied, just loud enough that Leon had to strain to catch what he said. "I go my boat."

"What?"

Miklos kept rowing.

"I go my boat."

Leon's exasperation showed again. "Come back. Where are you going?"

Miklos kept rowing.

"I go my boat. I go fish." Miklos stopped rowing for a moment. He gave Leon the finger and then resumed rowing out into the river.

Leon ignored it and gave up the conversation. He took out his frustrations on his men.

Miklos knew the river. When he reached the middle, he stopped rowing. He relaxed and let the flood tide take him up the river. Leon and his men had departed the riverbank to resume their search for Victor elsewhere.

Miklos again addressed the hull of the boat. "Men gone. We middle river. We drift up. We pass Piran Park and get to Cody Warne place with no row. Take two hours. You stay down for bit more. I tell you when okay."

The silence under the tarpaulin had started as a relief, but it evolved into one of those silences that no one wanted to break. One of those silences with blame attached. One of those silences that got deeper the longer it went on. One of those silences where you were afraid to move.

* * *

Thirty minutes later, Miklos invited them up from the gloom and dampness under the tarp.

"You come up. Safe now."

Up they came. Silence mercifully broken. They stretched their aching bodies.

"All okay, Miklos?" Victor ventured.

"All okay," Miklos replied.

The relief from the silence was temporary.

"No, it is not okay. It is fucking not okay. My home and business have gone up in smoke, and bad people are chasing us. All because you were fucking your so-called sister! It's not fucking Okay!" Athena shouted at the world.

"A—"

"Do not 'A' me!"

"A—"

Miklos started laughing. "I think you married."

Victor and Athena stopped the duel, and a more civilised silence descended. Victor contented himself with examining the contents of his swag bag. Miklos occasionally rowed the boat. It looked as though he was stretching rather than rowing, but the boat moved along nicely.

The evening light was starting to fade, and the tide was slackening.

"We not make main river channel tonight. We stop here or go backward when tide change."

Victor felt just a little deja vu. Back at Piran Park. But this time on the south bank.

Miklos rowed them into the shore. No pontoon, no sophistication. Just a scraping of the boat on the gravel told them they had made it.

All three of them disembarked.

"We need boat tomorrow?" Miklos enquired.

"We need it now. We need to sleep and have some shelter

for the night. We can trust no one but ourselves."

"It bit cosy!" Miklos observed after a moment or two.

Athena had no idea what they were talking about. Victor and Miklos seemed to her to have an understanding. An understanding of what each other was thinking. It was as if they had known one another for years.

Both men dragged the tarp out of the boat and laid it on the shingle shore of the river. They placed one of the backpacks at one end and the other two at the other. Then, they picked up the rowing punt and upturned it. It was a struggle, and Athena didn't help, as she had no idea what they were doing. They placed the upturned boat over the tarp, raised on one side by one of the backpacks.

"A cosy room for the night," Victor suggested.

"Really?" Athena sighed.

"Two sleep, one watch. I watch first," Milkos said.

Victor and Athena nodded and smiled at Miklos. Then, they clambered under the boat, their bodies separated by Victor's sack of high-tech, illegal goodies. The two of them were soon asleep, leaving Miklos to admire the reflections of the stars dancing on the ripples of the ebbing tide.

51

There was a gentle tap on the upturned hull of the boat. Victor was instantly awake.

"Miklos?"

"We change now?"

"Okay."

Victor quietly crawled out, and Miklos replaced him. Athena, deeply asleep, gently snored away at the night, undisturbed by the changing of the guard.

"Miklos. Pass out the bag. I need to have a play whilst you sleep."

Miklos passed the bag to Victor.

Victor opened the bag containing the tech and then looked at Miklos.

"Sleep," Victor instructed in the whispered tones they had been using so as not to wake Athena. Miklos nodded and disappeared beneath the boat.

It was a dark and clear night, but the city still exuded enough light for him to see by. Victor had the three packages in front of him. He had previously managed to get one of the MFBs to work and used it to help navigate the river. One of the packages he couldn't make do anything and he had given up.

He now turned to the third one. The one labelled "PJ07011927." The one that was supposed to be sitting in front of Kelvin instead of in front of him. He gently removed the protective packaging.

It was a sphere, just big enough to be comfortably held in both hands and not too heavy. Its surface had a brushed metallic finish and was silvery in colour. Victor held it in his right hand. Nothing happened. He held it in his left hand. Nothing happened. He cupped the thing in both hands, and it vibrated slightly.

The orb said, "Partial identity match to library."

Victor wasn't sure what to do. So he said, "Victor Atk—"

The orb replied before he had finished his name. "Identity confirmed."

The orb became crystal clear.

"Show the location of Kelvin Kraxler," Victor asked.

"Blocked," came the reply.

"Show location of Sienna Kraxler."

"Unable to provide accurate location. Within this radius." The orb displayed an orange ovoid shape overlaying a holographic image of the city.

"She is within the orange area?"

"Yes, orange volume," corrected the orb.

"Is she alive?"

"Yes."

"Can you improve the accuracy of her location?"

"Inactive for a long time. Yes, but it will take many hours."

"Start now."

"Yes," replied the orb.

"Repeat for Carlos Atkar."

"Yes."

"Repeat for Samantha Keogh."

"Not possible."

"Why not possible?" Victor said.

"She no longer lives."

Victor took a moment. Until now, he had hoped that his adopted mother was just missing.

"You sure of that?"

"Body biometrics logged at disposal facility within the city confirmed."

"Who disposed of the body?"

"Incomplete documentation."

"Can you show me the documentation?" Victor asked.

"Here it is."

Victor found himself staring at a blank form.

"It's a blank disposal form."

"It's the one that was submitted with the disposal."

Victor paused again and thought for a few moments before continuing.

"Show location for Leon Kraxler."

"Yes."

A small orange volume appeared on a hologram of the city.

"Inform me if Leon Kraxler comes closer than five hundred metres."

"Yes."

"Can you access the orb belonging to Kelvin Kraxler?"

"Yes."

This seems to be going a bit too well. Victor thought.

He ploughed on.

"Show me recordings of all activity in Kelvin Kraxler's office."

"Cannot display to you. Permitted only to Kraxler family."

"Can I re-access you anytime by holding you with both hands and speaking?"

"You only need to speak. Hands and voice are required due to a prolonged period of inactivity. Shall I listen for commands?" the orb asked.

"Yes. Can I add other users?"

"Yes, who?"

The two people with me. They are under the boat at the moment."

"I will listen and watch, and they will be able to use me fully. You need do no more."

Victor wanted to say thank you, but he knew it was just a machine.

"Thank you," Victor said.

"Good night," said the orb.

52

Leon turned away from the river and the old rowing boat. He was not a happy man. His father had given him one job. Recapture Victor. That's all he had to do. None of his men met his gaze. They all returned to the SUVs. Leon had just started the engine when his phone pinged. He turned the engine off and took the call. He knew he had to take the call.

"Dad, have you got any news?"

"No. But I'm hoping you have." Kelvin's voice came down the phone.

It was just about audible to everyone in the SUV. With the exception of Leon, all the occupants pretended to be deaf.

"We nearly had him. But he slipped through our fingers."

"Have you programmed an AI drone with his biometrics yet?"

"No. We got a tip from a good source and headed off to follow it up."

"So a big fat no and a big fat waste of time. Get back here and get it done."

"We should keep looking here for him. The AID can wait. I've been thinking about it. We trialled all the biometrics with the things. We loaded all the Kraxlers and Keoghs when we first got the AIDs. So it's all loaded already. All you have to do is activate it and choose what you want it to deal with?"

"You can do it," Kelvin said

"I know I can," Leon said.

"It was a statement. Not a question. Not an encouragement. Just get it done. Then we can leave it to do its thing on autopilot whilst we get other messes cleaned up."

"What other messes?"

"Never mind." Kelvin sounded tired.

Leon was tired, too, and it was starting to show.

"Dad. Who has the AID?"

"Plural son. We have more than one."

"Well, we have one less than we used to have because Victor lifted the thing from Cody just before I arrived."

"We have more. There are several on the eighth floor. They won't have the biometrics loaded, though. I'm in the building now. Get back here, and you can load and activate one." Kelvin instructed.

Leon did not immediately respond.

"Leon?"

Silence.

"Leon? You still there?"

"Dad. We might have a huge problem."

"Fuck sake, Leon. I have enough on my plate now."

"It's not a problem. It's a potential problem."

"Oh, I'm so relieved," Kelvin dripped sarcasm.

Leon said nothing. Kelvin said nothing.

Eventually, Kelvin said, "Get back here."

Leon considered his options. Tell his father now, or tell him later face to face.

It was a no-brainer.

"If Victor has our pre-loaded AID, then the whole family is at risk."

Before his father could process it and reply, Leon said, "On my way."

Leon hung up. He and his men headed back to the Kraxler building. Leon was the driver. He drove slowly.

He wanted his father to have calmed down, at least a little, from the rage that would have been brought on by the news of what Leon had told him over the phone.

Leon entered the building and headed straight up to see his father. His mood had swung from defence to defiance. His father was alone with a glass.

"Well. Fucking mess, Leon." Kelvin said, gently putting his glass down. He would be running short if he broke many more.

"I doubt—"

"Could we have been more useless?"

Leon opted for silence as the best reply.

"Leon. I have just been looking at some footage from intercept drones in a subway station, blowing holes in the chest of Victor."

"What! That can't be. Because I've just been chasing him around the city."

"I agree. It can't be, and it isn't. It's an interceptor drone killing an innocent bystander because Atkar's locator beacon had been removed and put in her clothing. And no sign of him on any cameras in the subway either."

Kelvin walked over to a screen and beckoned Leon over to join him.

"Look at this. This is the feed from the backup interceptor drone. Do you recognise this man?" Kelvin asked.

Leon looked. "He looks familiar. He's bleeding."

"You don't miss much, Leon," the sarcasm returned.

"Wait. I do recognise him. He's one of Cody's men. I think he's a medic or something like that."

"Fancy a trip to the lower levels?"

"Cody won't be any help finding Atkar."

"Let's find out what Cody knows about his guy with the bleeding arm and anything else connected to Victor," Kelvin said.

Leon headed for the door. Kelvin did not.

"Oh. I thought you were coming to the basement with me to interrogate Warne." Leon said.

"I'm busy. Very busy. You go. And get something useful from him. And quick."

Leon Kraxler arrived at the waterside basement of the Kraxler building soon afterwards.

"Mr Warne. Still here, I see."

"It seemed sensible to stay, Mr Kraxler."

"Agreed. Now, tell me who this man is." Leon showed him the picture of the man on the drone feed from the underground.

"Mike," Warne said, deadpan.

"Mike?"

"Medic Mike. Well, his real name is Paul. But everyone calls him Mike."

"Everyone calls him Mike?"

"Yeah. Exactly. Medic Paul doesn't really roll off the tongue. He should have been a priest."

"Priest Paul."

"Padre Paul sounds better."

"Enough!" Exclaimed Leon. Then a tardy thought jumped in, and he couldn't help himself. "So there must be a short word beginning with 'C' to go in front of 'Cody'."

Cody seemed too sharp for Leon today. "'Cabby'…it's got to be an occupation. 'Cabby Cody.'"

Leon reset his brain. "Mike works for you?"

Cody returned to deadpan. "Yep."

"What was he doing for you in Piran Park and the

subway?"

Cody decided on helpfulness. "I owed Victor a lot of money, and he wanted a favour."

"What favour?"

"He wanted his locator beacon surgically removed," Cody said.

"And Surgeon Simon did that for him."

"No, Mike… Oh sorry. I get it." Now Cody was not keeping up.

"He was supposed to, but nothing went well that day."

"I know that. We asked for our stuff that you were supposedly keeping safe for us, and Victor just walked off with it instead."

"Sorry," deadpan contrition was tricky to achieve, but Cody managed it quite well.

'Do we even know where Medic Mike is?"

"No idea. No idea, since I am currently under Kraxler house arrest."

"Okay. Enough of the medic. Let's talk about Atkar and the companion he picked up."

"What about them?"

"Cody. You need to be helpful rather than difficult. Even a neutral stance is pissing me off, to be honest, so let's get to it, shall we?"

"Atkar looked a bit battered… Black eye and bruises. He wasn't in prison kit, so he must have—"

"Don't think for me, Cody."

Cody couldn't entirely stop the duelling.

"He must have got his clothes from somewhere."

He realised how obvious that sounded as the words fell from his lips.

Leon just looked at him.

Cody continued. "The man with him was old and a sailor. He has his own boat—an old wooden thing. It probably leaks like a sieve, according to my men. It's not sea or river-worthy. Foreign accent, too. Not from around here."

The old wooden boat that they had torched for coming too close to the Kraxler building. Nice gaff-rigged thing. It was a shame to burn it. Isabella would have liked it.

"I think 'had' applies now rather than 'has.' The burned wreck of his boat is at the bottom of the river."

"So Victor and this other guy, the older guy.... they at the bottom of the river too?"

Alarm bells were increasing in volume inside Leon Kraxler's head.

"This old guy. What was he like? What was he wearing? What were his clothes like?"

Cody took the time to think about it, and eventually out it spilled. "Old, lined, and brown face. I think he had a thin white moustache. Hair was white, too. Well, what I could see of it was white. He was wearing a kind of black and white flat cap. It had frayed edges, which matched his hair. To be honest, it looked like he never took the thing off."

Leon said nothing. The alarm bells were now ringing too loudly. He could see the image of the man painted by Cody. He easily filled in the canvas's blank parts with a rowing boat and a raised middle finger.

Leon decided that it would be best all around if most of this information failed to reach his father.

"Anything else useful for me?" Leon asked.

"So it was useful then?"

"Anything else?" Leon's voice exuded impatience now.

"Don't think so."

"Okay. Time to go." Leon said, fed up with duelling now.

"Where are we going?"

Maybe one last thrust of the duelling sword.

"We?"

Warne went with it, "Where am I going?"

"Wherever you like."

"How do I get back?"

"Your choice," Leon said, followed for some reason by, "Rowing boat or Cab?"

Leon left Cody alone in the basement to consider his travel options.

53

Sienna woke first. She was no longer entangled with Carlos's body, but she was still very close to him. She rolled away and tried not to wake him. Unsuccessfully.

"Morning."

"Morning, Carlos. Thank you." Sienna said

"For what?"

"The Atkar hug."

"F.O.C.," he said.

"What?"

"Free of charge and special."

"Nothing is free of charge, and I definitely felt something very special!

"What?"

"Well! I felt something. It was pretty obvious what I felt."

"Sienna. That happens routinely to men in the mornings. It's called 'morning glory' and can happen with or without a companion."

"Oh? Really. I didn't know that. Why didn't I know that?"

"Sienna. Let's move on from that. It wasn't stirrings of passion, although if I were attracted to your sex, then you would obviously be up there."

"Carlos... Yes, let's move on from that."

"Good plan. This room, just like yesterday, does not smell of sex," Carlos said.

"Enough! We both know there was no sex and no desire. We have more things to worry about. We need coffee. Does this place do coffee?" Sienna asked

"Of course. The best brew is called Morning Glory!"

Sienna's look told Carlos all he needed to know about the suitability of continuing with the Morning Glory chat.

Sienna's face had changed at the sight of his discomfiture. She laughed out loud.

Carlos said, "Let's go get some coffee. Doesn't matter what it's called.

Thirty minutes later, Carlos and Sienna were sitting in the front window of Fanny's and Dick's, drinking coffee.

"We need two things as far as I can see," Carlos said. "Get out of the city and find Victor."

The coffee was making its presence felt on Sienna's neurotransmitters.

"Genius!" She sipped away at the coffee some more.

Carlos had no immediate response, so Sienna filled the vacuum.

"Next move then? Let's make a list."

Carlos remained silent. Sienna decided enough was enough.

"So, Victor will be leaving the city, too, if he can. Won't he? So if we head to where he's heading, we will have fulfilled both parts of our plan. So, where would Victor like to have his next morning coffee? You said Oakwood last night."

Carlos was jolted into speech by Sienna's tone and subject.

"He would go to Oakwood."

"Oakwood." Sienna prodded.

"Oakwood. Home. Home from before. Before…"

This brought Sienna up short. She had rarely heard Carlos

or Victor talk about Oakwood. Carlos's voice gave away the deep emotions that had been hidden for years.

After a few moments of silence, Sienna enquired, "You packed for the trip?"

The mood lightened.

"All ready. You?"

"All ready."

"Let's go south then. Let's go and find my Victor and your Victor. Let's head for Oakwood." Carlos said.

Sienna lifted her eyes from her coffee, looked at Carlos's face, and said, "You don't want to go to Oakwood, do you?"

Carlos gave an almost imperceptible shake of the head. He had had enough coffee.

"Come on. Bag grab time. Let's head to Oakwood. I think I remember the way." Carlos said.

Sienna finished her coffee, and soon she and Carlos were standing outside Fanny's and Dick's.

"It's shit like this that keeps the world alive," Carlos said.

"What?"

"Just stupid, fun, nonsense stuff. Like the name of this place. Stupid nonsense, but fun. But we need to get on with the non-fun stuff of life for a time. But we will return."

"To Fanny's and Dick's in particular, or to fun and nonsense in general?"

"Both. Both."

54

Sienna and Carlos left Fanny's and Dick's with their backpacks slung over their shoulders for the short walk to Carlos's car. The packs were thrown in the back.

"We'll drive part of the way back to my place and lose the car. Then we can head towards Isabella's and the south of the city on foot."

"I'm not sure that's a good plan." Sienna said."

"Why not?"

"Not sure. Just a feeling. That's where they would be looking for us. Let's go west and take the river road south, under the Vantuba cliffs. We might find some info about Victor on the way."

Carlos thought for a few minutes, his driving slowing.

"That way would take us close to the seafront family houses. You may be expected there."

They were silent for a while, and then Sienna said, "Okay, south to Piran Park, then cross the river and to Isabella's."

"It's a plan," Carlos said, directing the car towards Piran Park.

Thirty minutes later, they parked the car on the north side of Piran Park, grabbed their backpacks and wandered slowly and unobtrusively through the park toward the river. They reached Piran Pier and jumped into one of the waiting water taxis. Five minutes later, they were on the south side of the river in the district of Ervan. They did not notice the upturned rowing punt on the shoreline.

"Should we go to Isabella's?" Sienna asked

"Well, I vote no. We don't know who will be there," Carlos said.

"Well, I vote yes, but we won't stay or speak to anyone."

"Then what's the point!"

"Come on. It's a thirty-minute walk away. I know what I'm doing, Carlos."

They got to Isabella's house about an hour later.

"Stay here, Carlos. I'll only be a second." Sienna said.

"No chance. I'm coming. I might get Waffles!"

Sienna didn't dignify it with a reply.

She went into the outer courtyard and found what she was looking for.

"Still there!"

Sienna smiled and pointed at an empty terracotta flower pot sitting inside a second terracotta pot. Sienna went over, removed the inner pot, flipped it over, and replaced it upside down on the other one. Their rims matched perfectly.

"Come on. Let's get out of here."Sienna said.

"What was that all about?"

"Come on. I'll tell you as we walk. You sure you know the way?"

55

Isabella got up from her kitchen table and stretched.

Wine o'clock.

There was a bottle of red open from the night before.

Shame to waste it.

She filled the glass and decided that some air was in order. It was a lovely evening. She liked to wander around her garden at any hour, but the evening was her favourite time.

She left the house, headed out into the inner courtyard, and then around to the barns and outbuildings. The flowers were giving up for the night, closing their delicate heads until morning. She could hear the birds discussing sleeping arrangements in the branches of the trees towards the back of the house. After a few minutes, she reached the bench seat. It was nestled in complete privacy between two barns and surrounded by climbing plants and shrubs. It got the evening sun, although she was a little late for it on this occasion. It had just dropped below the wall. She tutted to herself, but the evening was warm enough for her to sit and take it all in.

It was her special place. She and her late husband used to sit together on the bench, his legs stretched out and her's crossed. Both clutching glasses of red wine, with the half-empty bottle scrunched into the gravel at their feet.

Sometimes, they talked about serious stuff, and the wine would seem to evaporate. Sometimes, they talked about less serious stuff; sometimes, they sat in silence. The wine still evaporated.

She always sat in silence now as she considered how the world had changed.

I miss him.

I miss Sienna.

I miss Connie.

I miss the kindness of people, once so common and now so rare.

I miss the children not being children anymore.

I miss the grandchildren not being children anymore.

She considered her glass.

One large mouthful, or two or three sips, remained. She stood and slowly headed back to the house without touching the wine.

Then she saw the flower pots and nearly gave the wine to the gravel path as an offering. Instead, with a shaky hand, she lifted the glass to her lips.

56

Isabella went straight into the house and picked up her phone.

She dialled Myra, who seemed to take an age to answer the call. Eventually, she picked up the call.

"Hi, Mum."

Isabella went for it. "You sitting down?"

"Why?"

"Sit down, My. I think I have some good news."

" I could do with some. Sitting."

"I think Sienna is alive and somewhere in the city."

"What! How do you know?"

"Flower pots."

"So now I know I am in an alternative universe! Flower pots!"

"Yes. Let me—"

"Explain."

"Grandparents and grandchildren have little private things going on. It's a fun thing that it's a secret between them. It's a fun thing that the parents aren't involved."

"So…"

"So. When Sienna was small, she wandered around my garden and discovered two empty pots stacked together near the outside wall. She went over and took the inner one out. She flipped it over and stacked it upside down on the other pot. Then she turned and caught me smiling at her. I went over to the pots, and Sienna watched me put things back as they were. She was sleeping over with me, and later that evening, I went for a walk around the garden. Sienna had changed the pots back again. When I went to say goodnight, we both smiled, and we both knew we had a new game. I stack the pots inside one another, and Sienna flips the top pot and stands it on top of the other."

"And…"

"And tonight, five minutes ago, I spotted it. The top pot is flipped. The top pot is flipped." Isabella said.

Both were silent for what seemed like ages.

Eventually, Myra said, "I need to tell Kelvin."

"Myra. Tell him face to face."

"I'll phone him now."

"Myra. Do me a favour, please. Please tell him to his face."

"Why?"

"Please."

"Okay, but why? He's at the office. He's always at the office."

"Because it would be nice for both of you. For both of you to feel the relief together. You never know. It might bring you a bit closer together. You have drifted apart a little, I think."

"Okay, but I need to go now."

"Thanks, My. I think it's the right thing.

Isabella cut the call, went back to the flowerpots and inverted the top pot once more.

57

The city's lights came on patchily. Only those areas with enough money to bribe the power company into routine maintenance had night lights. The Kraxler building was fully illuminated.

Kelvin was alone with his thoughts and his habitual evening drink.

The doorman buzzed up. "Mrs Kraxler is on the way up."

Fuck. Not now, he thought.

"Thank you," he said.

Myra didn't even knock. She went straight in.

"Kelvin," she said, beaming.

"What is it?" Kelvin said, totally put off by his wife's smile. Sour lemons seemed to have turned to sweet oranges, and she looked years younger for it.

She looked him in the eye and said, "I have news of Sienna. I think she is alive and around the city somewhere."

Kelvin was almost up to it. Almost. "Oh my God. That's... How do you know? What do you know?"

The words were the words she had expected, but the tone was slightly off. The look on Kelvin's face was the look she had expected, but slightly off.

"I think she's been to Isabella's... I think."

"Has your mother seen her?"

"No, I don't—"

"Well, how can she know!" Kelvin's tone had changed—just a hint of aggression.

Myra just looked at him, unsure of something. She found a chair. Kelvin didn't.

Kelvin's tone changed again. "I won't be happy until she is back with us."

"Yes. Yes, I know Kelvin. I agree. But still. It's good news, right? It's the only news we've had in ages.

"Tell me all you know. Then I can get my men on the case ASAP."

Myra told him about the flower pots.

"Flower pots! Fucking flower pots! You are basing all this optimism on fucking flower pots!"

You have such a way of making me feel small. Myra thought.

"It's something! It's a lead! What are you going to do?" Myra almost shouted the words at her husband.

Kelvin forced himself to calm down. He walked over to his wife, took her in his arms, and held her tightly. "We will find her," he said.

He let her go. "Sorry. It was a bit of a shock. It's fantastic news. I will get busy getting our teams out that way. See what they can find."

"Okay."

"You want to stay here, or are you going to go home?"

It was meant as, and had the air of, a dismissal.

"I think—"

"I need to get on this now, Myra."

"Okay. Keep me up to date, won't you? See you later?" Myra said.

Kelvin had already turned away.

Myra headed home, just in case Sienna headed there.

58

Mason and John headed down the street away from The Orange Room Club. Mason's dramatic pulmonary performance stopped almost immediately.

"So you work at that club?" John asked.

"Not any more," Mason said.

"So I save you from a burning building, and the only information you will give me is your new employment status."

"What do you want?" Mason asked.

"I need some help finding someone, and I need some weapons."

"Who do you need to find?"

"Sienna Kraxler," John said.

"Sienna Kraxler! Her father has the whole city looking for her."

"None have looked very hard. She has just killed my brother."

"What! Where? When?"

"Never mind," John said.

"Seems to me you know more than I do."

"I need help working out where she would go rather than where she has been."

"Why should I help you anyway?"

"You ungrateful bastard. I could have left you to burn back there. Maybe we should count it as a reprieve from burning rather than a full-on saving thing. If you don't help me with this, I will arrange for the flames to be relit under your sad ass."

"Okay. Chill." Mason said.

"So?"

"Come on. I'll take you to someone who might know."

Cody was back in his office and not in the best of moods. He had had no sleep the night before and was struggling to understand how his fortunes had taken such an adverse turn.

There was one man in the office, ostensibly guarding Cody.

Cody addressed him. "Get those two useless articles in here, and Mike too."

It took the guard a moment to realise that "articles" could mean people as well as things, and off he went on his mission. This meant that no one was guarding the door when Mason and John arrived.

Mason gently knocked on the door and got no reply. He stepped back from the door, not daring to knock again.

John elbowed Mason out of the way. He didn't knock, opened the door and addressed the occupant.

"Good morning, Mr Warne."

Cody did not recognise the voice as he looked up from his desk.

"And you are?" Cody asked.

"I am a potential customer. A potential enemy and a potential friend."

"Let's do the customer bit first, shall we? I'm not sure if I want you as an enemy or friend, but a customer will do."

"You know where I can find Sienna Kraxler?" John asked

"You want to be a customer? No one knows where she is."

"I know where she was a couple of days ago, but not now. So do you know anything about her location, or not? I will pay."

"I'm afraid not. So there you have it. An honest response to encourage some honest dealing."

"Okay. So my next question… can you provide me with a rifle with telescopic sights?" John asked.

"Silly question. Of course, I can."

"Price?"

"Depends what you want in the cross hairs."

"Well, that's my business."

"Can't sell you one if any Kraxler is a target. Be very bad for business."

"Okay. No Kraxler killing." John promised.

"Guaranteed?"

"Yes, guaranteed."

With no minions to help him, Cody took some time to locate the required item and the accompanying ammunition. Back in his office, the financial arrangements were concluded.

Mason was still hanging around and achieving nothing. He could see nothing advantageous for himself, so Mason decided to stir things up a little.

"He will kill Sienna. If he can find her. She killed his brother."

Cody looked at John. "You lied to me!"

"No, I didn't," John replied

"You said you would not kill Sienna"

"I made that deal with you. I will not kill her."

"What will you do to her then?"

"I will not kill her."

Cody considered this for a moment.

"What will you do to her then?" Cody asked.

"I will not kill her. We had that deal, and I will stick to it."

Mason was still getting nowhere. "What's in this for me?"

Cody and John looked at each other and said nothing. Cody looked down at his desk, and John turned and left. Mason stood, unsure of what to do. By the time he decided to follow, John had gone, his new gun slung over his shoulder.

59

Cody was glad to see the back of Mason and John despite the fact that he had made a tidy profit on the rifle and ammunition. He was still waiting for his men to come to him. The two men who had been locked in the container by Victor and Miklos. He was also interested in hearing about Mike's adventures, and misadventures. All could wait, though. He was glad of the peace. He leaned back in his chair and put his feet on the desk. He closed his eyes. Tiredness from the preceding sleepless night overtook him, and sleep took him elsewhere.

The door to Cody's office opened quietly, and a man stepped in and approached the desk. The man had greying red hair and a drooping left eyelid. His unsmiling face looked down at Warne. He firmly prodded Cody's boot with the barrel of a rifle, sending the owner's feet to the ground. Cody was instantly awake.

He looked up at the man holding the gun. "Who the fuck are you?" Cody said.

"Never mind who I am. We have work to do."

"I work for myself. Why would I work for you?" Cody said. It was more of a statement than a question.

"We will work together. And we will work together for our employer."

"I am not employed by anyone."

"Let's cut the crap, Warne, and get to it. Everyone in this city works for Kelvin Kraxler. We just do different things for him. Then we are rewarded, or punished, as he sees fit. That is how it works, and you know it. Pretend you have control over what you do if it makes you feel better, but let's cut the crap between us."

Cody paused to consider the implications of yet another intrusion into his office.

"What work?" he said.

"Search and rescue work… of Sienna Kraxler."

"She's been missing for ages. Why are you barging into my office now?" Cody asked.

"Because it has suddenly become a top priority for our boss. The top priority."

"Well, he hasn't asked me to do anything other than look after some of his stuff."

"Well, I'm asking."

"Yes, but I ask again, who the fuck are you?"

The man with the gun paused and considered.

"My name is Floyd."

"And what's in it for me?"

"Being in Kelvin Kraxler's good books. But mainly being in mine." Floyd stared unsmiling at Cody.

"Uh. Okay. What do you need from me?" Warne said.

"You got any information or ideas about where she might be?"

"She's a popular woman today. Already had someone else looking for her."

"Who?"

"No idea. But he is very keen to find her. Says she killed his brother. Wants revenge."

"Shit. And how is he going to do that?"

"Probably shoot her."

"And you know this how?"

"Well. I sold him a gun." Cody said.

"Not putting our boss's daughter in any danger then. Idiot. What gun?"

"Automatic rifle with telescopic sights."

"Well, our first job will be to find him," Floyd said.

"Or we find Sienna first. You know that Victor Atkar is out of Vantuba prison, too, don't you?"

"Not really interested in Victor Atkar any more. My job is to find Sienna Kraxler and keep her safe. You are now my official helper."

"Uh, okay…" Cody said doubtfully.

"I have my ideas as to where she would go. What about you?"

"Not thought about—"

"Well, now's your chance to think about it," Floyd said.

"She will head to her family. Her sister. Maybe her mother or grandmother. Probably not Kelvin or Leon. Don't think they got on overly well. She may go to Atkar. There have been rumours about the two of them."

"So, where is Connie Kraxler?"

"I hear she is in the mountains to the south of the city," Warne said.

"So she will head south and into the mountains? If she does, she will pass her grandmothers on the way through. That will be our first stop, then."

"We don't have to both go, do we?" Cody almost pleaded.

"Yes, we do. The quickest way to the old lady's house is by boat up the river. And you have fast boats and some reasonably competent help. Come on. Let's get to one of your boats," Floyd said.

Cody reluctantly got up from his seat and joined Floyd in

heading for the door. Before they could leave the office, Mike strode in with his arm bandaged.

"Medic Mike?" Floyd said.

"How do you know me?" Mike asked.

"I know lots of things. It's part of my business."

Cody looked impressed.

"Mike. You are coming with us. You may come in handy." Floyd said.

"Where are—"

"Doesn't matter. Come on. We are leaving now. Bring your kit," Floyd said.

Mike grabbed his medical backpack with his good arm and slung it over his shoulder.

60

Victor felt damp rather than cold. Dew had formed on him whilst sitting under the stars. Athena and Miklos still slept under the upturned boat on the riverbank. The black of the night sky was in the process of surrendering to the oncoming day, and the tide was once again on the flood. He tapped the upturned hull of the boat. A few moments later, Athena appeared from beneath, looking dishevelled but still with a twinkle in her eye. Miklos was slower to appear, and he always looked dishevelled.

Miklos looked at the river.

"We go by boat. Now good time," Miklos said.

"But where are we going anyway?" Athena asked.

"I am going home," Victor said.

"Home? They will find you and lock you up again," Athena said.

"No. Not my home here in the city. My old home. My parents' home."

"Where home?" Miklos asked.

"Small village south of the city. Good land. Good land for farming. Good land for lots of things. That's why we were forced to leave years ago. I can go on my own. You two need not come with me."

"Stay till paid," Miklos said.

"You owe me a nightclub, Vic. So I'm staying until I'm paid, too," Athena said.

"Tide!" Miklos reminded them, looking at the river.

The three of them righted the upturned boat and dragged it down to the waterline. Victor and Athena got in, and Miklos pushed them out and started to row them out into the channel. He rowed gently for about half an hour, and all three of them watched the city landmarks slip by behind them.

"Hear that?" Victor said.

"It fast boat," said Miklos.

"Must be rich, powerful, or both to afford the fuel," Victor said.

"Not friends," said Miklos.

"We're in more shit then," Athena said.

All three of them were looking over the stern of the rowing boat at the approaching inflatable boat.

"Two minutes, and they'll be here. We will end up in the river!" Athena said.

"What we do?" Miklos asked

"You and Victor get under the tarp. I'll row. No one is looking for me." Athena said.

They changed positions in the boat. Athena rowing—well, holding the oars at least. The seat with the protruding nails attacked Victor, as he and Miklos covered themselves with the tarp. Victor kicked out at it in pointless revenge. Athena could see the inflatable almost on them. She kept rowing, in the middle of the river channel, the tide on her side pushing her along. The power boat approached them at speed and very close to them. It showed no sign of stopping.

"Hold on! They are going to tip us over with their wake!" Athena shouted into the boat, but her words were drowned out by the engine's noise.

The rowing boat rode up the wake and toppled down the other side, the starboard side scooping water into the boat. Athena instinctively adjusted her weight and just managed to prevent the thing from tipping over. Then, the second wave of the wake hit them. It had less of an impact, but it put more water in the boat.

The inflatable did not stop. It turned as if for a second pass. Athena recognised the man standing at the controls. It was Cody Warne, and he was enjoying himself. There was another man, sitting in the boat, whom she didn't recognise.

61

Cody was enjoying himself. He was pleased about it, too. He had been strong-armed into coming along on this trip, and so he was going to make the most of it.

Floyd was getting wet in the bow of the inflatable. The river was choppy, and Cody was at full throttle. So was the boat. He spotted the rowing boat and headed straight for it.

Floyd was in his own world and only noticed the rowing boat at the last moment, just as Cody cried out, like a small child, with the fun of it all.

They passed the rowing boat.

"Go back!" Floyd shouted over the engine noise..

"Why?"

"That woman doesn't know how to row. And she is out here in the middle of the river. Go back."

Cody needed no encouragement to keep going with the fun.

"Crack on!"

He turned the boat around and headed back again at full speed.

"Slow down," Floyd instructed.

Cody pretended not to hear.

"Slow down now and come alongside," Floyd said.

Warne reluctantly obeyed and throttled back. The nose of the boat dropped, and the sudden deceleration caused the motor wash to climb into the back of the boat.

"You alone?"Floyd said to Athena.

Athena chose defiance, her default setting, "What's it to you? Little boys playing in a big boat. Nothing better to do?"

"What's in your boat?"

"Me!" Athena said with a distinct note of irritation.

"Anything interesting under the tarp?" Cody chipped in.

"Quite a lot of water since you two assholes drove by."

Floyd lifted his gun and pointed it at the floor of the wooden boat.

"How many holes do you want in your boat?"

He fired a single shot at the floor of the boat.

There was much wriggling from beneath the tarp. Victor and Miklos appeared from beneath it. Unscathed.

Athena continued to sit and hold the oars. Victor was on his hands and knees, and Miklos had made it to his feet.

"Victor, how nice to see you again," Warne said.

Victor nodded.

Warne continued. "How the tables have turned. You two have stolen from me and, well, stolen from Kelvin Kraxler, actually. And I have been blamed. I need that stuff back. You got it with you in the boat?"

Floyd looked at Victor and cut in, "Do you know where Sienna might be?"

Victor shook his head and looked blankly back at Floyd.

Floyd nodded at Victor. "I am not really interested in this sideshow, but I will almost certainly be back for you, Atkar."

Floyd turned to Cody. "Come on. We have more pressing things to attend to. We need to find Sienna, or the man with the gun, looking for her. Let's go," he said.

"Wait. I want my stuff?" Warne said.

"I have a score to settle, too." Mike raised his bandaged arm to Victor.

Floyd raised the gun, but he was unsteady. Both boats were swaying and jerking in the choppy waters.

"I'll get your stuff for you. Here it is." Victor said.

He grabbed the bag and, hidden beneath it, the piece of wood at which he had been directing his frustrations earlier. He stood up and made to give the bag to Warne. Then, he appeared to lose his balance, and he fell forward towards the inflatable. He dropped the tech bundle back into the rowing boat and nearly ended up in the river.

He scrambled for the inflatable and swung his right arm around, looking like he was steadying himself.

The section of the old seat containing the nails struck Floyd in the calf and knocked him off balance. Floyd fell to his hands and knees, steadying himself on the tube of the inflatable. Still holding the gun, Floyd tried to right himself, and he started pushing himself up on the tube. Victor swung the wood again, this time into Floyd's hand. Floyd let the gun go, and it fell into the river. He didn't cry out. Victor used the nail and wood again. This time to puncture the tube. He then scrambled backwards into the rowing boat. Miklos pushed the two boats apart with his foot, and Athena started rowing towards the south bank of the river.

"The boat is taking on water. We need to get to the shore." Victor said.

"We make it. It not far. Same for them." Milkos said.

"Good job a strong woman is rowing us," Athena said.

"Try and go in straight line," encouraged Victor.

He was looking over the stern of the boat at the inflatable, which was limping its way carefully to the opposite shore.

"Who was the man on the boat with Cody?" Victor asked.

"No idea," Athena said.

"Same," Miklos said.

"I know him from somewhere. They are not following us. They are probably heading back to Warne's place. They will be back on our tails soon, though, I expect. We need to put some distance between us."

Athena was quick to react. "You want to row? Be my guest, Victor."

He smiled back at her and said, "Sorry, A."

He drifted off into himself and whispered to no one in particular, "I know him."

62

Isabella replaced the pot as it had been before Sienna interfered with it. She decided another call to her daughter was in order. Myra picked up almost immediately.

"Myra, are you okay?" Isabella asked.

"I'm fine. Just excited, that's all. Sienna is alive and somewhere in the city. I know it now."

"Get some food on. I'm coming around to see you. What did Kelvin make of the news?"

"Well, he was pleased, but something wasn't right," Myra said.

"Is he at home?"

"No, he's at the office, as usual."

"See you in about thirty minutes then," Isabella said.

"Mum. She is alive, I know it!" Myra said.

"You've cooked. Now we need to eat." Isabella instructed.

"Pasta. Sienna's favourite."

"Myra. Get a grip. It's a hint that she is fine, but just a hint. It may well be a message for us, but she isn't here with us yet. We need to sit and talk this through calmly."

"How can I be calm when my missing daughter might be

found?" Myra complained.

Isabella sighed. "Serve the food. Maybe wine, too? It will help our brains work things through."

Mother and daughter stared at each other, but the older stare had more behind it. Years more practice gave it the right intensity to get the job done.

"Sorry, Mum. Let's eat."

Both women tucked into the food wordlessly. Nothing was left on the plates.

"Myra. We need to think this through now. Sienna has been away for a long time without a word. That means that she has either been kept away from us against her will, or she has decided to keep away from us herself, or she is dead."

"She's not dead!" Myra exclaimed.

"My, calm down. I don't think she is either, but I don't think she would have left us voluntarily without saying a word. So, let's run with that. It means she was taken and kept away from us by someone, but has now managed to leave us a message."

"The pots?" Myra said.

"The pots," Isabella confirmed.

"Who would take her?" Myra asked.

"It doesn't matter. What we need to figure out is where she is or where she is going."

"So?"

"Coincidences, My."

"Coincidences?"

"It might be a coincidence, but it seems weird that Victor was imprisoned for Sienna's disappearance, and he has just escaped. They were close, weren't they?"

"They got on really well. Maybe too well." Myra said.

"So why would he harm her?"

"And why would he harm Sam? She was like a mother to him."

"Maybe he didn't harm either of them."

"He was found guilty."

"Yes, but Kelvin let it be known around the city that Victor should be punished for it if he was guilty. He put more weight on the 'should be punished' bit than on the 'if' bit."

"Maybe, but he just wanted to blame someone. His daughter was… is missing."

"We don't know where she's been or where she is now. We do know there is a link between Sienna and Victor. We know where he has been. We don't know where he is, though."

"Or where he is going," Myra added.

Silence fell for a few moments. Then Myra asked, "Where would Victor go?"

"Where would you go, My?"

"Home," Myra said.

"Home. But which home? He can't go back to his home here. He would be caught and locked up again."

"So his old home. Where he came from. Oakwood, it was called. But I think the place was abandoned."

"Still home though, My."

"So you think Victor is heading to Oakwood? That's not finding Sienna, though?"

"No, it's not. But if Sienna somehow knows Victor is out, she may have reached the same conclusion as us. And the news of Victor's escape is everywhere in the city," Isabella said.

"So you think Sienna might be heading for Oakwood?"

"I think it's the only thing I can think of. It kind of makes sense. It all hangs on a coincidence, though, and I don't like coincidences."

"They do sometimes happen," Myra said.

"Only one way to find out."

"Well, let's go. We are fed and watered. Let's go. I'll just tell Kelvin."

"My. Let's just the two of us go. Kelvin is busy here. Maybe we should get Connie to join us there. She would be closer anyway."

"Uh, Okay. You will have to speak to Connie. She never answers my calls."

"I'll try her now. Let's head to Oakwood as soon as I've spoken to her."

Isabella headed off to make the call. Myra found an old-fashioned paper map and included it as part of her backpack packing. She packed little else.

"We will never make it before nightfall," Myra said.

"No. I think you're right," Isabella said. "Leave a note for Kelvin. Tell him you'll be staying at my house for a few days. We shall stay there tonight and make an early start in the morning."

"Okay, but a very early start. I can't sit around and do nothing."

63

They got the rowing boat ashore without too much difficulty. They were all wet and cold but unscathed.

"You really don't need to come," Victor told Athena and Miklos. "We could all have been shot back there."

"I come till paid," Miklos said.

"You owe me a club," Athena confirmed.

"Okay. We will have to walk. It's a bit of a climb, I think. And we will get wet. Well, wetter." Victor encouraged.

Athena and Miklos looked at each other. Athena said, "Once you're wet, you're wet."

All three smiled and set off along the riverside towards Oakwood.

As they walked south, Victor spotted the wall he and Carlos had slept against the first night they had come to the city. It seemed to him both like yesterday and a lifetime ago. He leant over to touch it.

"Last time I was here, I slept against this wall with my brother," Victor said.

"How long will it take to get to your village?" Athena asked.

"All night and some of tomorrow," Victor said.

Miklos chipped in, "It late. Go tomorrow."

"I need to get out of the city. Everyone is looking for me," Victor said.

"We could stay in a safe house… somewhere really safe, like The Orange Room," Athena dripped sarcasm.

Victor just looked at her.

"Okay. There was no need for that. Sorry. Actually, I do know somewhere close by where we could safely stay. There would be no questions asked," she said.

"Reliable and loyal staff?" Victor returned the sarcasm.

Athena shrugged. Miklos said, "Sleep. Then go tomorrow."

Tension relieved, Victor said, "Lead the way, A."

An hour later, they were sitting around a table, drinking and eating at the back of a busy bar.

"Fanny's and Dick's?" questioned Miklos.

"Don't ask," said Athena.

Victor was not in the mood for verbal niceties. "I think we should head upstairs and get our heads down. We have an early start tomorrow, " he said.

"One more drink," Athena suggested with a degree of force.

She attracted the attention of a barman, and he came over.

"What can I get you?" he said.

Before any of them could answer, the barman asked, "You Victor Atkar?"

Victor looked at him and said, "Why?"

After a few seconds, the barman looked back at him and said, "Well, if you are Victor Atkar, your brother was here yesterday. Well, today, actually. He left this morning with a redhead lady. Not his usual type, if you know what I mean!"

Victor said nothing and kept his face blank. The others did the same.

"And if you're not Victor Atkar, then your brother, if you have a brother, was probably not here," said the barman.

Victor neither confirmed nor denied his identity but ordered the drinks instead.

"Another round of these," he said.

The barman went about his business.

Victor said, "It has to be Sienna with Carlos, and we need to leave now. I have been recognised."

"I think you're right about Carlos and Sienna, but we don't need to leave. This is a safe house. Good and reliable staff.", said Athena with a look on her face that challenged anyone to bring up the recent events at The Orange Room.

"Why were they here?" Victor asked her.

"I should think Carlos comes here quite a lot and not just because it's a safe house. How should I put this, Victor? This is the sort of place that is suited to his social set. It's the best bar for his social set in the city."

"How did I not know that?"

"Because it's not your sort of place, is it?"

The drinks arrived. The barman made no further enquiries of his guests and departed about his business elsewhere in the bar.

"They must be heading for Oakwood, too. Carlos would think it a safe place, even with what happened there when we were boys. Good places to hide. Eyes everywhere in the city." Victor said.

"Or he was with a random redheaded woman in a bar that mostly caters for same-sex couples, and that bar just happens to be on the route from Carlos's place to the road out towards Oakwood. No brainer." Athena said.

"Okay. We go now. Catch up." Miklos said.

"No. We drink and sleep, and then we start early tomorrow." Athena instructed.

64

Sienna and Carlos left Isabellas' house and began the long walk to Oakwood. Sienna told Carlos about the flower pot game she used to play with Isabella as a child.

"She will know I did it," Sienna said.

"What will she do?"

"Hopefully, relax and tell everyone else that I am Okay. Carlos… I need time to think about what to do. I killed a man."

"You killed a jailer. And you didn't mean to.."

"The end result is the same, though."

They continued on in silence for a while, deep in their own thoughts.

"Is it far to your old home? It's getting late." Sienna enquired at last.

"We will probably have to walk through the night and most of tomorrow morning."

"No one knows where we are, and we are safe as long as it stays that way. I have an idea." Sienna smiled.

"Go on, tell me," Carlos said.

"Isabella will know that I have been at her house because of the pots thing, but she won't expect me to stay in the guest quarters. There is an outbuilding at the back of the house. She will think I've gone off somewhere again. Let's turn back and stay there tonight. Then we head off to your old home early tomorrow. What do you think, Carlos?"

"I could do with some decent sleep, to be honest. Same for you, I expect. Okay. Let's do it. Lead on."

Quietly, they retraced their steps. They made their way around to the back of Isabella's property. There were no lights on.

"The key is normally here," said Sienna, lifting an upturned clam shell from the doorstep.

"Super security," Carlos said sarcastically.

"Yes, and once inside, we will put the key back in case Isabella comes looking."

Carlos was getting tired. "You're in charge. Let's go in."

65

Myra and her mother had an almost silent supper. The air was full of tension, unspoken worries, and hopes. They soon headed to their respective bedrooms for an early night in preparation for an early start.

Isabella fell asleep quickly and deeply. Her daughter did not.

Myra left her bed, dressed, and headed out into the night. Although her mother had told her not to, she couldn't help but tell Kelvin.

She took one of the cars through the city towards the Kraxler building and made it there without incident, parked and went in.

"Good evening, Mrs Kraxler," said the guard on the door.

"Hi. Mr Kraxler in?"

"Yes. I'll let him know you are here," he said.

"No, don't worry. He is expecting me," Myra lied.

Myra took the private elevator to Kelvin's rooms on the top floor.

The doors were not locked. She gently knocked and went in without an invitation.

"Kelvin?"

Just the slightest of hesitations before Kelvin said, "My!

What are you doing here so late?"

"I just needed to see you to tell you what's happening. We are going to find Sienna first thing tomorrow. Isabella and I are leaving to find her south of the city." Myra said.

Kelvin stood and looked at his wife. "Go on," he said.

We think she is with Carlos, and they are heading to Carlos's old home village. Oakfield or something like that. We think she must have met up with Carlos, and that he is taking her there for safety. Will you come with us, Kelvin?" Myra asked.

Kelvin was slack-jawed for a moment, and then, almost in a whisper, he said, "Oakwood."

"Pardon," Myra replied.

Louder this time, "Oakwood. Oakwood was the home village of the Atkar boys."

"So, will you come with us?"

"You, Isabella, and I will be slow. We should get my team to head to Oakwood to find them. They will be much quicker. We can follow everything from here."

"Are you sure?"

"Let me make the call. Back in a few minutes once I've sorted it out."

Kelvin left Myra and went into the next-door room.

"Floyd. It seems likely that Sienna and Carlos Atkar are heading for Oakwood. You remember Oakwood?" Kelvin started the call.

"I remember," Floyd said.

"How quickly can you get there?"

"We are in the south of the city now. We will probably need to walk. I will leave first thing in the morning. It is too dark to negotiate the footpath now. If we do not get there before them, it won't matter. I will sort it out."

"I want Sienna returned to the city and put back in the penthouse flat. And this time, get some competent guards to keep her there. I need time to sort out the endgame on this." Kelvin said.

"You don't want me to sort the end game out for you now?"

"No. Sienna is not to be harmed. Just get her back where she belongs."

"Consider it done," Floyd said.

Kelvin quit the call and headed back to speak to Myra.

She had already left the room and was almost out of the building.

Myra wasn't sure she had heard it right.

It's difficult when you can only hear one side of a conversation.

She was outside the Kraxler building now, driving herself back to Isabella's. Back to what she hoped would be the safety of her mother's house. She thought about whether to take the back streets or the main thoroughfare—back streets after dark or the direct route where she could be spotted more easily.

Soon, she gave up thinking and just drove. The paranoia that every sound and every movement was hostile kept her focused on the drive.

66

Carlos was awake before it was light. He turned to Sienna, with whom he had once again shared a platonic bed, and gave her a gentle shake.

"What?" she said sleepily.

"It's time."

Sienna came instantly awake.

"Okay. Let's get going. Quick toilet moment, and then we go." Sienna said.

After their early morning needs had been attended to, they grabbed their bags and headed out into the very early dawn.

"One sec," Sienna said.

She made for the flowerpots. They were grey and dark in the corner of the garden, but she could have found them with her eyes closed. She grabbed the upper pot and inverted it as she had done so many times before—another message for Isabella.

Then, the pair left the house. Sienna followed Carlos along the road as they headed further south, out of the city. In the dim light, the river on their right looked oily black as it headed in the opposite direction.

"Let's keep off the road as much as possible, just in case," Carlos said.

"It will be slower off the main route, though."

"Are you in a rush to get somewhere or in a rush to stay safe?"

Try as she might, she couldn't sleep. Myra got up and headed for her mother's room. She knocked gently and then went in.

"Mum," she said softly.

There was no response.

"Mum," louder this time.

Isabella turned and looked up at Myra.

"What time is it? I know we said we would leave early. Have I overslept?" Isabella said.

"No, it's early, really early, but listen to me. This is important, and I don't understand."

"Understand what?" Isabella asked.

"I'm sorry, Mum, but I couldn't not tell Kelvin about us going to find Sienna."

Isabella was fully awake now.

"You told him?"

"Yes. I went to the Kraxler building and explained everything to him. He said we would be too slow following Sienna because you are old. He said he would get his team to find her and Carlos."

"Old and slow!" said Isabella with a frown. "Let's see, shall we?"

Isabella was out of bed and dressing for the day.

"Wait, Mum. That's not all. I heard Kelvin phone someone about Sienna. I know I could only hear Kelvin's side of the conversation, but I don't understand."

"I told you not to tell Kelvin."

"I know. But he is her father. He should know about things. I don't understand what he was saying. It doesn't make sense."

"Tell me what you heard, Myra."

Myra noticed that her full name was used rather than the truncated, more friendly form.

"He said, '*I want Sienna returned to the city and put back in the penthouse flat. And this time, get some competent guards to keep her there.*'" Myra said.

"What?"

Myra repeated it and added," What did he mean? I don't understand. Mum?"

Isabella remained stoned-faced and silent for a time. Then, when she spoke, it was quiet and determined.

"My, come on. We will get to Sienna before your husband's team. Old and slow. I don't think so. Come on, My, I want to show you something."

Grateful to be referred to in a friendly way, Myra said, "Where are we going? We need to get to Sienna!"

"That's what we are going to do. I need to tell Connie, too. I'll do that now. Wait here." Isabella said.

Connie took the call from Isabella.

"Connie, how are you?"

"I'm good. Just heading back to the farm. Make sure all is well there, and then back to the mountains. Are you okay? You sound a little off."

"You know the country south of the city? Do you know a place called Oakwood?"

"I've heard the name. It's where Carlos and Victor came from, I think. Why?"

"Do you know where it is? Can you get there?"

"My little bundle of illegal tech can tell me. Again...Why?"

"I'm with your mother now. We think Sienna is heading there with Carlos. It's complicated, but I don't think it would be safe for you to go back to the city. Your mother and I are going to Oakwood now. Safety in numbers, maybe?

Sienna told me not to come back until she tells me it's safe."

"I think she meant not coming back to the city rather than not leaving the mountains."

"Um, okay, but I need to go to the farm first. Then I will head to meet you."

"Good. But be careful. I'm not sure what's happening here, but I have a bad feeling. There are some bad people out there. Trust no one."

Isabella cut the call and returned to Myra. Connie consulted her multi-function bulb for directions to Oakwood.

"Come on," Isabella instructed her daughter.

Isabella led the way out of the house and around to one of the outbuildings. "Let's hope it starts, " she said.

"What starts?"

"In here," Isabella said, indicating an outbuilding.

"I've never been in there. It's always been locked."

"Yes, well, parents can have secrets. They also were young once and occasionally disobedient."

Isabella turned the key in the wooden door, and the mechanism clicked.

"Go on. Open the door."

Myra stepped forward and opened the door. In the dimmest of early morning light, she could just about make out the shape of a bike.

"Mum. A motorbike!"

"Less talking, My. Let's see if we can get the thing started."

Isabella mounted the bike, and after several attempts, the machine sputtered into life.

"Get on the back, My. Put your arms around my waist and relax."

Neither of them was particularly relaxed as they set off from the house. Neither was sure how the day would turn out. Neither of them was sure that riding a motorcycle was a good idea.

"You get the helmet." Isabella handed it to her daughter. "I only have one."

As they sped out of the house, Isabella just caught a glimpse of the flowerpots.

67

Floyd, Cody and Medic Mike got aboard a new inflatable at Cody's compound and, within minutes, were heading up the river. They would have to double back on foot a little to get to Isabella's, but the boat sped them on their way.

Floyd brought the boat alongside the jetty and quickly secured the bow. All three men came ashore with their various loads.

"Let's assume that if they have left Isabella's house, they will be heading south out of the city, probably on the main road. If we head from here to Isabella's, they will have to pass us."

"What if they have already left the city?" Cody asked

"Then we will know soon enough."

There wasn't much traffic, and not many people around. It was still early. The three men walked abreast along the road, spread out as if they didn't want to keep one another's company. They walked at a decent pace, looking down every side street in search of Sienna. The city was quiet.

"We must almost be at Isabella Lightfoot's place", Cody broke the silence.

"No sign of her. No sign of anyone." Mike said.

"Can you hear that?" Floyd asked.

"What?"

"It's the sound of a motor. It's coming this way." Floyd said.

The motorcycle came towards them, carrying two people. An older lady was driving, grey hair blowing in the breeze. The pillion passenger looked younger, but it was hard to tell with the helmet covering the head. Mike and Cody moved to their respective sides of the road, leaving Floyd at the centre. He stood still and watched as the motorcycle chicained past him.

All three turned to look at the receding pair. The couple on the bike did not turn.

"Did you recognise them?" Floyd asked.

The other two shook their heads.

"Bit unusual, though. Know any old women with motorcycles?"

Heads continued to shake in the negative, either side of Floyd.

The three of them pressed on towards Isabella's house. When they got there, they found no one in residence.

The door to one of the outbuildings was slightly ajar.

Floyd made it more so and went inside.

"We missed them. They were on the bike!" he said.

"Who?"

"Lightfoot, and probably Myra Kraxler."

"What now, then?" Cody asked.

"We missed them. They were heading south. We need to follow them. They must know things we don't."

"But we don't know where they are going, do we?" said Warne.

"Come on, we have a long walk," Floyd said.

68

The road had become a track. Little more than a path. Isabella stopped the motorcycle.

"Off," she instructed her daughter.

Myra wordlessly obeyed. Isabella also dismounted, turned the front wheel to the left and sent the machine onward into the bushes.

"Now we walk," Isabella said.

"I had no idea you had a motorcycle. Never even thought you would be able to ride one."

"Your father was mad keen on the thing. He taught me how to ride before you were born. I kept it up secretly after he died. I probably have lots of talents that you don't know about."

"Probably," Myra replied.

Mother and daughter walked on in single file along the footpath, hugging the riverbank.

"My, what do you think Kelvin is up to?"

"I don't know. I don't understand what I was listening to. It sounded like he was telling someone to capture and lock up our daughter. How can that be? There must be another explanation."

"Or… Or it's true."

"You've never really liked Kelvin, have you?"

"To be honest, Myra, no, I haven't. And as the years have slipped by, I have come to like him less and less. Now, I wouldn't put anything past him."

"Even locking up our daughter?"

"It is hard to conceive that even Kelvin Kraxler would do such a thing." Isabella paused and consulted her paper map.

"Okay. Time for us oldies to do a bit of climbing." Isabella said.

In the distance, they could see and hear a large waterfall. They headed south towards it, then began the climb to the higher ground beyond.

They followed the footpath and climbed past the waterfall. They didn't stop to eat or rest, and the hours slipped by. They passed through dense woodland. Eventually, they left the wooded expanse of trees and could see the village of Oakwood in the distance.

The fields surrounding the village were overgrown. Partially constructed houses were scattered around and also overgrown with weeds. Bulldozers and other construction vehicles were abandoned in the fields. The only sign of habitation was a whisp of smoke from the chimney of one of the older-looking houses.

"Is this the place? Is this Oakwood, where Victor and Carlos lived?" Myra asked.

"I think so, My. They might be here already. They might be in that house with the smoke."

"Or not. There might be people here we don't want to meet."

"Only one way to find out, Myra."

Isabella strode off towards the smoke. Myra followed quietly. They both stopped outside the door to the house and looked at one another. Isabella, as ever, took the lead and knocked on the door. There was no reply. She knocked again. Still no reply. The two exchanged another silent glance.

Isabella put her hand on the door handle and turned it slowly. She pushed the door open. It creaked on its hinges. The inside of the cottage was dim, and a small fire burned in the hearth against the back wall. Next to it was a small chair occupied by a fragile-looking old man. He looked as if he hardly had the strength to hold the gun that he was pointing at them.

"What do you want?" His voice was quiet but firm, with not a note of concern.

"We are looking for Victor Atkar and his brother, Carlos. They used to live in this village, I think." Isabella said

"Lots of people used to live in this village," came the reply.

"Do you know Victor and Carlos Atkar? Is this Oakwood?"

"Who are you?" said the old man.

"Victor and Carlos used to live with us in the city. They managed to escape from here when bad things happened years ago."

The old man said nothing and kept the gun steadily pointing at the women.

Eventually, Isabella broke the silence. "Do you know the Atkars?"

Once again, the old man said nothing for a while.

Eventually, he broke the silence. "There used to be an Atkar family here."

Myra spoke to him for the first time, "Where is everyone?"

"There is only me here. Most of the villagers were forced to leave. Those who didn't leave wished that they had."

"Do I know you? You look familiar." Myra asked the old man.

He didn't reply.

"What happened to you?" Isabella asked.

"I ran away like a coward."

"But you're here," Isabella said.

"I came back. No one was left. Just me."

"Where is the Atkar house?" asked Isabella.

"Who are you?" He asked again.

"We told you. We are looking for Victor and Carlos." Myra said."

"That's not who you are. That's what you want. I know what you want, but don't know who you are."

Myra started to speak. "My name is—"

"Isabella Lightfoot, and this is my daughter, Myra."

"Now I know your names… but I still don't know who you are."

Isabella countered," Do any of us really know who other people are?"

Before he could reply, she asked," Do you have any food? We could do with some food."

The old man was good at silences, but eventually, he cracked and said, "Some, but not a great deal. I can spare you a little."

His offer coincided with him lowering the gun to the tabletop at his side. He levered himself out of the chair and walked, stooped, into the kitchen at the rear of the cottage. Isabella and Myra followed him.

69

Carlos stopped walking and turned to Sienna.

"I'm not sure I want to go any further. That's Oakwood."

"We've come a long way, Carlos," Sienna encouraged.

"I don't think I can go back there," Carlos said.

"Maybe the ghosts should be laid to rest just as the bodies have been." Sienna realised that this sounded harsh. She reached out and took his hand, gently at first and then more firmly. She led him forward towards the village.

"There's smoke from one of the houses. Someone is here." Sienna said.

"It might be Victor?" Carlos asked, almost childlike.

"Yes, it might. But it might not."

She pulled him forward again, and they headed into the village. As they approached, they could hear muffled voices from within. They could also smell cooking.

They reached the front door and looked at one another. Carlos seemed a little more settled now that he was actually in the village rather than just intending to be.

"Do you know this house, Carlos?" Sienna whispered.

"No."

"Shall we go in then? I am hungry."

Carlos considered it for a moment and then said, "There is

a saying that hunger always wins in the end."

Sienna turned, knocked on the door and stepped back, putting herself between the door and Carlos.

The muffled voices stopped.

They strained to listen and could hear shuffling footsteps heading for the door. The foot shuffling stopped.

"Come in," came a voice from within.

Sienna pushed open the door and looked straight into the barrel of an old man's gun. She gently pushed Carlos back.

"More visitors! I haven't had anyone here for years, and now you're knocking on my door. That's four people in one day. Who are you?"

"My name is Sienna Kraxler."

The old man lifted the gun to his shoulder, shuffled forward and pointed it straight at Sienna.

"A Kraxler!" The old man almost hissed.

His finger pressed more firmly on the trigger.

Sienna said nothing but did not flinch from his gaze. The old man shuffled closer to her.

"A Kraxler! You—"

From behind the man, Myra calmly said, "Not all Kraxlers are the same."

The old man spun around, aiming the gun at Myra now.

"You only told me your first name. Let me guess. You a Kraxler, too?" he said.

Isabella responded before anyone else. "Not all Kraxlers are the same," she said.

"You a Kraxler too?" he said.

"I told you my name is Lightfoot."

The old man looked around him and seemed to notice Carlos for the first time.

"You a Kraxler too?"

"No. My name is Carlos Atkar. I come from this village."

"Atkar? What is a man from this village doing with a

Kraxler!"

Carlos stepped forward and put himself between the gun and Sienna.

"These are good people, whatever their names. They took me and my brother in when we had nothing. My father was killed in a house along the road from here. My mother was raped and then killed. The men that attacked us left us to die here. We escaped, and these people, Kraxlers, looked after us."

"Still Kraxlers! Destroyed our village for money and didn't even finish the job."

"So. In your house right now, you have two Kraxlers, one local man, a woman and yourself." Isabella had decided to intervene.

"Carlos and his brother Victor managed to survive the massacre in this village, but I have no idea how you survived?" Isabella continued.

The old man seemed to hesitate, and he started to lower the gun.

"I was a coward," he said.

"How were you a coward?" Isabella ploughed on.

The man suddenly looked even more hollow. He looked around at them all. The anger at the Kraxler name was replaced by a look of self-loathing. Tears moistened his cheeks.

"I was on the other side of the village when the men came, when the drone things came.. My family was here in this house. I heard the guns. I heard the screams. I saw the fires. I did nothing to help. I was rooted to the spot. A coward. My family. Dead. Except me, the coward. I knew my family was gone, so I left the village, but it pulled me back. I had to come back. I found my dead family and buried them. By the time I came back, the village was completely deserted. I couldn't leave again. I will die here and join my dead family."

The gun in his hand shook slightly. Myra and Sienna walked toward each other and embraced—a long, long overdue embrace.

Isabella watched and smiled. Then she turned back to the old man.

"We all make decisions in life. Some turn out to be good, and others bad. Each one, though, conscious or not, is made with the intent of it being a good decision." Isabella said.

A sadness hung in the air—even the crackling fire seemed to emit no heat.

The smells from the kitchen eventually defeated the sad air, and the old man offered the newcomers food.

Carlos said, "I cannot eat yet. There is something I must do first. Somewhere I must go."

Sienna said, "I will come with you. You were there for me when I needed you. I will come with you."

"No. I need to go on my own." Carlos said. "I will come back here when I'm done and eat from this kind man's table."

Carlos turned and left. The others headed for the kitchen.

70

As Carlos closed the door behind him, Sienna turned to her mother again and gently shook her head.

Myra went to her and hugged her again. Tears of relief ran down the cheeks of mother and daughter alike. After some time, Myra pulled away and looked at Sienna.

"Tell me," Myra said.

"You won't believe me. You won't believe… it."

"Well, tell me anyway. If it's okay with our host," Myra looked at the old man, "let's sit while you tell us your story."

The old man nodded his approval, and they sat.

Sienna told her story. The faces of her audience registered differing emotions. Myra's face depicted total disbelief. Isabella's features expressed anger. The old man's face was hard to read, but he mostly looked sad.

Myra looked at her mother questioningly. "How can this be?"

"People sometimes end up in places that they never intended to visit. Looking back, some can see the ill-judged turning points in the road. Others look back and can't see where they lost their way. Some never look back. Whichever applies to your husband, he has ended up in a very dark place. Dark and unpredictable. We need to be very careful."

Isabella said.

"It explains the conversation I overheard on the phone?" Myra seemed to ask the room, but only Isabella knew what she was talking about.

"It does indeed," Isabella said.

71

The three looked out over the village from the forest's edge. It had been a long day, and Miklos wondered if the trip was worth it. Athena was of a similar mind.

Victor also had reservations. His primary concern was not returning to Vantuba prison, but history and the apparent safety of home had pulled him here. Long and short friendships, along with the hope of material gain, had brought the other two along for the ride.

"Place look empty," Miklos said.

"The place looks destroyed! Most of the houses are in ruins. There is smoke from one of the houses. Not my house." Victor said.

"No nightclub?" Athena asked

Victor said nothing.

Miklos followed Athena's vibe. "No old boat? No new boat?"

Victor ignored them, deep in thought.

"I'm going down to my old family house. It's time." Victor set off toward Oakwood without another glance at his companions.

Miklos and Athena wordlessly looked at each other and fell in behind Victor. They had come this far with him. They would see this through to the end with him.

It took them about twenty minutes to walk into the village and to get to Victor's old house.

"Here it is," Victor said.

"You left door open when you left?" Miklos asked.

Victor stepped forward to the door. It was slightly ajar. He glanced at the other two, stepped forward, and pushed the door open.

Carlos was sitting in their father's chair. Tears were rolling down his cheeks.

"Carlos? What are you doing here?" Victor said gently.

Carlos turned to him and said, "It will never be okay."

"It will be okay, but it will never be the same," Victor said. He clasped his brother's hands, pulled Carlos from the chair, and hugged him. The brothers stood there in silence, holding each other.

Carlos eventually broke the embrace, held his brother at arm's length and looked at him.

"I know you didn't kill Sienna."

"I know Carlos. You have always stood by me. You always believed me."

"No. I *know* you didn't kill her."

"What?"

"I know because she is alive and here in Oakwood."

"Where?"

"She is a five-minute walk away. In an old man's house with Isabella and Myra."

"Why—"

"Why not ask her yourself?" Carlos said.

Athena chipped in, "I think that would be a good idea, Vic."

"Can you two give us a moment?"

Athena and Miklos quietly left the cottage and found somewhere, not entirely engulfed with weeds, to sit.

Carlos sat back in his father's chair. Victor couldn't sit.

In a gentle voice, Victor asked, "Do you think we should look around the place?"

"I can't do it. I want to do it, but I can't. I see Mum and Dad everywhere I look."

"I know… Carlos, I think we have two choices. Look around and accept the nightmare, or leave now. Just sitting here agonising is no good." Victor was firm but gentle, still looking after his little brother.

Carlos smiled a watery smile at Victor. "Just a couple more minutes of agonising. Then we will go.

Carlos left the chair, and the two brothers glanced once more at their boyhood family home, then turned and left with Athena and Miklos in tow. They headed for the smoking chimney.

72

Kelvin was not a happy man. Usually in control of everything, he now seemed to be in control of nothing. He needed an update. And he needed a drink, even though it was early. He put in a call to Leon.

Leon let it ring as long as he dared, but his father's persistence eventually paid off.

"Dad?"

"Update!"

"No luck with finding Victor. Cody was no use. It seems Victor was holed up in a nightclub called The Orange Room, but he slipped through the net and got away to the river."

"And what are you doing personally?" Kelvin asked.

"My men are searching the city," Leon lied.

"And you?"

"I am coordinating."

"You are useless!" Kelvin cut the call.

Kelvin went to the drinks cabinet and poured out a long drink that should have been short and should have been kept for later in the day. He called Elliott.

"Elliott, any news about Atkar?"

"Kelvin. No news about Victor, no. We have drones

programmed to find him searching all over the city, but nothing."

"Leon thinks he was at a club called The Orange Room, but that he then escaped to the river."

"Okay. I will redirect the drones to search the river. Are you in the office?"

"I'm always in the office," Kelvin said.

"I will redirect them."

"Thanks, Elliott. Keep looking. We know Atkar had something to do with Sienna's disappearance.... And maybe Sam's. We need to find him." Kelvin drank some more.

"Kelv—" Elliott said as Kelvin cut the call.

Kelvin finished his drink and replenished it. He called Floyd.

"Have you found her?"

"No," Floyd answered as he walked away from the others.

"Where are you? Do you know where she is?"

"We are on our way to Oakwood."

"We?"

"We. Myself, Cody Warne and one of his men, a doctor."

"And you know where she is, Floyd?"

"I think so. It seems she went to Carlos when she escaped, and they both headed for his childhood village of Oakwood to get out of the city."

"How far away are you?"

"Probably another hour or so. Should be there just before dark."

"Once you have her, lose your companions."

"Lose them?"

"Yes, lose them."

"No mess."

"Exactly. Get back to me once you have her." Kelvin cut the call.

* * *

Kelvin tried to call his wife, but to no avail.

She is probably with her interfering mother, he thought.

His drink was finally hitting the spot, so much so that he considered the unthinkable.

He tried to call Isabella to see if Myra was with her. Again, to no avail.

Connie never answered his calls. He could see where she was if he used the locator functions on the tech that she took everywhere.

"Trekking or farming," he thought.

He grabbed his multi-function bulb to check. The MFB could only tell him that Connie was not at her farm or in the mountains.

Alone in his office, Kelvin was not a happy man.

73

Carlos knocked on the door of the little cottage with the smoking chimney. He pushed at it, and it opened with ease. Tentatively, he put his head around the door. The old man was once again sitting in his chair at the fireside, but this time, he had no gun at his side.

Carlos looked at him and said, "More hungry people for you to feed, I'm afraid."

Carlos turned and beckoned the others to follow him. Victor was the first of Carlos's entourage to enter the room, followed by Miklos and Athena.

"Sienna!" Victor beamed.

"Vic!"

They ran to each other, embraced and kissed in the middle of the old man's cottage.

"What a glum lot," Athena commented. "Should you not all be happy?"

The old man asked, "I think I'm gonna need a bigger house. Are any more people coming?"

Everyone rudely ignored their host.

Victor said, "She's right. We should be happy. What am I missing?"

Myra said, "I think you should tell your story again."

Victor looked at Sienna, and she told her story again.

"He killed Samantha!" Victor almost shouted it at her. His disbelief was so strong. Carlos found a seat.

"Yes. And I don't think he knew what to do once I found him out. What could he do? Kill me, too? Explain it away. Outright deny it? I think he imprisoned me until he could decide what to do. But that didn't give him any more options. Just gave him a bit more time"

Myra went to her daughter and hugged her again.

"It is true! It's also true that I killed one of my guards when I escaped. I didn't mean to. It was an accident. I was desperate. It was an accident."

The room once again fell silent.

"It's okay," Myra said, continuing the hug.

"It will never be okay," Sienna said.

"It will never be okay," Carlos agreed.

"I will make it okay, but it will never be the same," Victor said.

The little cottage was full of people, and the old man looked a little stunned by their presence.

"It will be dark soon. We must stay safe through the night. We don't know who might be looking for us," Victor said.

"Kraxlers on the loose!" said the old man. "Might not be safe anywhere."

"This kind old man is overwhelmed with strangers in his house. At least some of us should go elsewhere." Victor suggested.

"Where?" Isabella asked.

Victor looked at Carlos. "Victor and I will go to our old house. It will be good and bad for us, but we should do it. There is room there for others, too. Sienna?"

Victor smiled a proud smile at his brother.

"I need to stay with my family, here," Sienna said.

Athena noticed that Victor now looked slightly hurt. Not one to miss an opportunity, she plunged in.

"Miklos and myself will come with you and Carlos," she said.

Sienna turned to the old man and asked, "Please, can we stay here while we decide what to do?"

The old man nodded his approval.

Victor led his brother and the other two out of the house and headed for the family home.

74

Floyd remembered the place. He remembered the last time he was here. He remembered leaving two boys in a house with their dying parents. He remembered the house.

"This way. I think we will find what we are looking for over there, " Floyd told Mike and Cody.

"Why not go to the house with the smoke? At least we know there is someone there," said Warne.

"It's a hunch. You ever get them, Warne?" Floyd delivered the question without humour, and Cody decided not to reply. Mike also kept his own counsel as the three men headed into Oakwood.

For once, the man with the gun was glad to be alone. John used to be a people person until his brother was killed. He looked around and could see no one. The village was almost deserted. He lay prone and lifted the gun sight to his eye, and his finger closed gently onto the rifle's trigger. He was no marksman. He had rarely fired a gun. He had difficulty holding the gun steady. The view through the sights jumped around. He could just about keep the crosshairs on the little cottage window from whose chimney smoke was rising. He could see the occupants of the cottage clearly enough. He knew who they all were, except for the old man. He wished him no harm.

Maybe I should get closer. He thought and lowered the gun.

He looked around again to see if he could move closer to the cottage without being seen. There seemed to be no one else in the village, but there might be lots of people inside their houses.

Now. Do it here and now. The worst case is that I will have to try again at another time and place."

He brought the gun back up to firing position. He could see all three women through the sight. His finger pressure increased steadily. The view remained a dancing field in front of his eye.

Multiple shots shattered the silence in the village of Oakwood. The glass of the old man's window shattered. Screams escaped the cottage through the shattered window. John dropped the gun. By the time he had picked it up and looked through its sights again, the view through the cottage window had changed. He couldn't see Sienna Kraxler. He couldn't know if he had avenged his brother.

75

The shots rang out across the village.

"Shit!" shouted Floyd.

He began running as fast as he could towards where the gunshots had come from.

"You two get to the cottage with the smoke and check out the occupants," he ordered.

Mike and Cody were not keen to move.

Floyd stopped. He turned and levelled his gun at them. "Now," he ordered.

They moved. Floyd turned again and headed off towards where the gunshots had come from.

"I will catch you up." He shouted over his shoulder.

If it were me, I would head back to the woods for cover. He thought

Mike and Cody were not the only ones running towards the smoking chimney.

Victor was the first through the door, followed by his younger brother. His eyes met a very pale Isabella, clutching her right arm in the old man's chair. Sienna was on the floor, with her mother on her knees, leaning over her. The old man stood silently, looking out of the window.

"Sienna! Sienna?" Victor said.

"It's her leg. She's been shot in the leg. Myra was pressing her hands down onto her daughter's left leg. Crimson oozed between her fingers.

"Belt or rope. Come on. A belt or a rope," Victor shouted.

Myra went to the old man, removed his belt, and went straight back to her daughter. She gave the belt to Victor, who quickly pulled it tight above the wound. The crimson oozing slowed and eventually seemed to stop.

Victor looked up and around the room. The old man was embroiled in a battle with his trousers and gravity. Isabella sat pale-faced in the old man's chair.

"Are you hit, too?" Victor asked.

"Yes, but I'll be fine. The bone is fine, and it's not bleeding much now."

Cody entered the cottage and saw Victor on his knees. Victor looked up at him just as Mike came in behind Warne.

Victor ignored Warne and addressed Mike. "How are your suturing skills?"

"Better when I can use both hands!" Mike showed Victor his recently sutured forearm.

"Sorry about that. Please, can you help?" Victor pleaded.

There was only a moment's hesitation before Mike went over and kneeled at Victor's side.

"I need scissors to cut the trouser fabric. I need to see what we are up against. Warm, wet towels are also needed to clear the view," Mike said.

The old man shuffled off to the kitchen and returned with the scissors and towels.

Sienna looked pale and clammy. Mike cut the trouser leg and used the fabric to wipe the wound.

"Can you lift your leg?" Mike asked.

Sienna managed to oblige, but it was painful.

"Good, so it looks like your femur is not fractured. The wound should be explored, but without full medical backup, we could easily make matters a lot worse," he said.

"Stop talking and start doing," came Sienna's instruction.

Mike opened his bag and started work.

76

Floyd made his way to where the shots came from. He found five empty shells on the ground. He also found footprints heading back into the woods.

Much easier to find the shooter than to try to find a Sienna in hiding. If it's not too late, thought Floyd.

He stopped and listened. He wished he had younger, more acute senses. He had experience, though, and he let that asset guide him in his search. He walked quickly and quietly through the woods.

He was almost back at the river and had not sighted the shooter.

Probably younger and fitter than me.

He stopped and listened again. He could hear the river but nothing else.

Then, another thought crossed his mind.

What if two people are working together to get Sienna?

"Shit!" He shouted to the trees.

He turned and headed back towards Oakwood in the fading light. He could feel events starting to overtake him.

77

Medic Mike had closed the entry and exit wounds with as many sutures as he could manage.

"Okay, now the tricky bit."

Mike turned to Victor, who was holding the belt.

"Very slowly, loosen the belt. Very slowly. We don't want bleeding into the muscle. Let's just see what happens."

Victor did as instructed.

All eyes were on Mike's suture lines.

After about thirty seconds, he said, "Release it a little more, Victor."

He did so.

"It's looking okay, I think. How does it feel?" Mike asked.

"How do you think it feels!" Sienna said with unnecessary anger.

"Sorry… Better now the belt is off," she said in an apologetic and grateful tone.

"Do you feel pressure?"

"A little?"

"It's not really bleeding now, but she's not moving her leg. Do you have any bandages in the house?" Mike said to the old man.

"No. Sorry," he replied.

"Do we need bandages?" Myra spoke at last.

"We need to put a pressure bandage over the wounds just in case of any rebleeds."

Victor slowly got to his feet. He returned the belt to the old man, whose trousers were glad of the extra support.

"Thank you so much," Victor said as he looked around the room.

"Maybe some bandages at our house," said Carlos, "We didn't use them when we were last here. It was too late."

"Yes, Carlos. I'll get them. Fifteen minutes or so," Victor said.

Victor turned to leave, then turned back and approached Isabella, who was still sitting in the old man's chair.

"How are you?" Victor asked.

"I am an old boot," she replied. Some colour had returned to her face.

Victor turned again and headed for the door.

As he left, he heard Mike say, "Fluids. We need to get some fluids into her. Water? Milk? Whatever you have."

The old man left for the kitchen as Victor closed the door behind himself.

78

Connie Kraxler was a strange mix. She loved the mountains, her farm, and its animals. She liked being alone for long periods, but didn't like being away from her family for too long. She also loved some of the tech gadgets that had recently been made illegal.

She held one of those gadgets in her hand now. It was a multifunction bulb. An MFB. It was top of the range, too, and completely illegal to possess. The Kraxler family was powerful, though, and no one would step out of line to bring attention to it, let alone bring down any legal sanctions upon her. She knew her father had one too, which never left his office, and her brother Leon had one but never used it.

She didn't use hers often, but when she did, she immersed herself in it. She liked the challenges of learning the intricacies of how it functioned.

Currently, it was guiding her through the increasing gloom toward Oakwood. It was guiding her to the front door of Victor and Carlos's old family home. Isabella hadn't told her where to go once she got to the village, so it seemed sensible to her to make that connection. The door was slightly ajar. She pushed on the door and stepped in.

"Hello?" she said.

"Hello… Connie?" came back at her from the upper floor.

"Victor?"

"Connie. What are you doing here?"

"No! What are you doing here? You are supposed to be a jailbird."

"Connie, we need to go and see Sienna, Myra and Isabella."

"Where are they?"

"Connie. I'll explain it all later. Sienna and Isabella have been shot. Isabella is Okay, but I must get these bandages to Sienna."

"Shit, Victor. What's going on?"

"I'll tell you once we get back to Sienna. Come on. It's only about five minutes away."

79

Victor had taken the lead on the short trip back to the old man's house. Connie hadn't stopped asking questions, but Victor had said little. As they approached the door to the cottage, Connie darted in front of him and barged straight through the door. Sienna was lying on the floor with her head on a cushion, Mike on one side and Myra on the other. There was no sign of Isabella or Miklos. The old man was in his chair, and Cody stood beside the fire. Just watching events unfold.

Connie gazed at the scene, open-mouthed.

"Where are the others?" Victor asked as he took the bandages over to Mike.

"Isabella and your friend Miklos have gone upstairs to rest," said Mike.

"How are you, Sienna?"

"Sore! Bloody sore. Bloody and sore," she said.

Victor looked at Mike, who nodded and gave a faint smile.

"Let's get those bandages on. We don't want to be going backwards here," Mike said.

Gently but firmly, the medic applied them. Sienna didn't complain.

"Will someone tell me what the fuck is going on!" Connie

exclaimed.

"I will tell you all about it, I promise," Victor said.

In a quieter voice, Sienna said, "No, you won't. I will."

80

Connie looked at Mike.

"Are you a doctor? Is she going to be alright?" she asked.

Mike replied, "In that order, definitely and probably."

"Fine. Thank you," Connie said, and she turned to Sienna.

"Come on then, big sister, tell me, please, what the hell is going on?"

Sienna started to explain in a gentle voice.

"The last time I saw you. We had been to see our father. Well, I saw him, and you didn't. I saw what he had done. I didn't want you to see. I didn't want him to think that you knew. That's why I got you away so quickly."

"But what had he done?"

"He killed Samantha."

"What!"

"He killed Samantha. Then, he locked me away in a luxury apartment overlooking the city. I was guarded day and night. Then I killed one of my guards and escaped."

"And I got locked up in Vantuba prison," Victor said.

Connie ignored Victor and concentrated on her sister, "How can that be true? Did you see him do it? Maybe it was just him finding her body."

Silence lay in the air. Sienna closed her eyes.

"It was him," Sienna whispered.

Mike said, "She needs to sleep."

He and Victor looked at the old man.

"There is a spare bed upstairs. It has not been used for years. It will do,' the old man said.

Victor and Mike looked at each other. Despite all that had gone between them, it seemed that any hostility or animosity had faded away.

"We can't all stay the night here. Will you stay with her? Please," Victor asked Mike.

"I will."

"I know," Victor said.

Victor took control.

"Please, can we use your house for tonight? Just until we get ourselves sorted out. I will repay you."

Athena said, "You are in debt to many people already."

"Debts will be paid soon enough," Victor replied.

"Athena, Miklos, Carlos, Connie, and I will sleep at our old house. Sienna, Myra and Isabella will accept this good man's hospitality. Mike will stay here, too, in case the wounded need attention." Victor instructed.

"I don't work for you, and neither does Mike," Cody said.

Victor sighed.

"Cody, how did you ever manage to get on in life? Can't you feel it in the air? Can't you work it out based on what you have heard here this evening? Things are changing. Tides are shifting. Be on the right side in the morning. And in case you hadn't realised, you are homeless tonight. There are lots of empty houses in Oakwood, though." Victor's voice was cold with menace. He had lost all patience with Cody.

Cody did not respond. Mike gave Victor the faintest of smiles.

Victor glanced at the old man, who gently nodded his approval.

"Vict—" Cody said

"The right side, Cody, and maybe don't wait until morning to get there."

He turned to Mike and said, "Let's get Sienna upstairs."

81

The domestic arrangements were sorted out in about fifteen minutes. Victor had stayed at the old man's house when the others left. Before he left, he wanted to make sure Sienna was doing fine.

The old man, Mike and Victor gathered around the fire. The Aged looked comfortable in his chair, gun still at his side.

"Thanks, Mike," Victor said. "No hard feelings?"

"No—I still have hard feelings, but, as you say, the direction of the wind has changed. Also, whatever the wind direction, I am a medical man, and my patients come first." Mike responded.

"Fair enough," Victor said.

"More debt to be repaid?" asked the old man.

"Old debt rather than more debt," Victor clarified.

The front door opened without a knock. Floyd strode into the house and looked around. He had a gun in his hand and something on his mind.

"Where is Sienna Kraxler?"

Victor looked at him and took a step towards him.

"Where is Sienna? I won't ask again."

"You don't look very happy," suggested Victor.

"I will be happy when I have Sienna back where she belongs."

"Will it make you smile?" asked Victor.

Without knowing why, Floyd smiled at Victor. The crooked smile was the last piece of the jigsaw, joining the greying red hair and the slight droop of the eye. Victor had seen it before.

Victor turned his back on Floyd and smiled at the old man.

"She is upstairs with her mother and sister."

"That was almost too easy, Victor Atkar. Sienna Kraxler, please."

"Upstairs. Do what you have to do."

Mike was making a good attempt at invisibility.

Floyd made for the staircase.

Victor went to the old man's chair, back still to Floyd.

Floyd had made it to the third stair tread when the shot from an old-fashioned shotgun peppered the back of his legs. He turned as he fell, not crying out, and levelled his gun at Victor. The shotgun was still pointing at Floyd.

"It's double-barreled," Victor quietly pointed out.

"I know," said Floyd.

"What shall we do? You shoot me? I shoot you? We both shoot each other? Or we stop for a while and chat? I don't have to aim to kill you. All I have to do is squeeze the trigger as I fall to the ground. You, on the other hand, have to make a kill shot. Wounding me would still leave you dead."

Floyd was grimacing, not smiling, now. "Shall we talk?"

Isabella's face appeared at the top of the stairs. Victor gently shook his head, and she retreated out of sight.

Floyd was struggling to reach any degree of comfort on the stairs.

"Mike, please could you take both our guns out of our reach, starting with his," Victor said.

Floyd could see he had little choice and handed his gun to Mike. Victor then did the same. Mike withdrew from the stairwell and returned the shotgun to the old man. He kept Floyd's gun.

"You been to Oakwood before?" Victor asked Floyd.

At first, Floyd didn't seem to understand the question.

"Have you been here before?"

Floyd thought, *Things have slipped way beyond my control. I am probably a dead man unless I know what this man wants.*

"I have been here before." Floyd played for time, desperately trawling his memories for a lifeline.

"Why were you here before?"

"Business."

"Kraxler business," hissed the old man.

"Kraxler business," agreed Floyd.

"When were you here? What was the business?" Victor asked calmly.

"Kelvin Kraxler wanted everyone out of the village so that he could get hold of the land and develop it for himself."

"Kelvin Kraxler!" The old man seemed about to reach boiling point.

Victor calmly went over to the old man and repossessed the shotgun. He gave it to Mike.

"Sounds like you might want to use it," Victor said.

The old man wilted.

"So… just business?" Victor addressed Floyd again.

Floyd elected for silence.

"No pleasure?"

Floyd said nothing, but the intensity of his gaze on Victor deepened.

"Uh? No," Floyd was floundering now, and he knew it.

"Stand up," instructed Victor.

"I can't!"

" Try. If you can't, I will drag you, not very gently."

"Where?"

"The thing is, it wasn't just business, was it?"

"What?"

"I get that the business of emptying a village for Kelvin Kraxler must have involved a degree of coercion, but…"

Victor let the silence hang there like a rope around Floyd's neck.

"It was business," Floyd pleaded.

"Memory returning?"

Silence again. Floyd was playing for time.

"Walk or be dragged? Up to you. But you will end up in the house where you raped my mother, killed her and my father, and left myself and my brother to die," there was a tremor in Victor's voice now.

Floyd, grasping at straws, said. "What about Sienna?"

"What about Sienna?"

"Where is she?"

"Upstairs, I told you that."

"Is she okay?" Floyd asked

"She's fine," replied Victor, but his reply was a split second too late.

"Shot?" Floyd said

"She's fine!"

"Window shot in and the person on our most wanted list is having a late afternoon siesta," Floyd said, seeing an opening. "We need to work together. There is still a gunman out there."

"That was you!"

"No. My task this time around was to bring Sienna back to Kelvin's safekeeping in the city. If she is hurt, then I have failed."

"Then you have failed, and there is someone else out to harm her."

"Her or someone else in this house, but probably her," Floyd said.

Victor went upstairs and was not overly careful with the obstruction he encountered on the stairs.

82

Victor got to the bedroom. Isabella clutched her arm in a chair at the foot of the bed. Myra was at the bedside holding Sienna's hand. Sienna's eyes were closed, but it felt like a deliberate act of exclusion rather than one of exhaustion.

"How is she?" Victor asked the room.

"What the hell is happening down there? More gunshots!" Isabella said.

Myra looked terrified.

"How is she?" Victor asked.

"Sore. Sore but fine." Sienna said.

"Sienna, do you know of anyone who would want to hurt you?"

"My father isn't brave enough. He would have killed me before now if he'd had the balls. And he would have blamed you."

"He might have changed his mind once you escaped. I don't think so, though, because he sent someone to get you back to the city unharmed." Victor said.

"Victor. I killed one of the men who regularly guarded me. Imprisoned me. There were two of them who worked together. They were brothers. I killed the one called Phil. His brother's name is John."

"Would he come after you?"

"Would you go after someone who had killed Carlos?"

"Or any of my family," Victor said flatly. He got up and returned to the ground floor, again, with little care for the obstacle.

Victor left the house without a word.

83

Victor made it through the deepening dusk to his former home. He didn't knock.

"Change of plan." He announced.

Connie was sitting with a disconsolate-looking Carlos, and Miklos was chatting with Athena.

"Why? We are basically in a deserted village in the middle of nowhere. Why do we need a change of plan?"

"Who shot Sienna and Isabella?" Victor asked rhetorically.

Silence.

"I think it was one of the guards who used to keep Sienna captive in the city. She killed his Brother."

"So, the change of plan is?" Athena asked.

"However cramped, I think we should all be in one place. If the gunman comes back to Oakwood tonight, he might go to either or both houses. They are the only places showing signs of life. We can't protect both at once."

"It good plan," Miklos said.

"Come on, let's go while there is still some light," Victor said.

With some trepidation, the others gathered up their things and headed off in train behind Victor.

* * *

John could see lights in two houses from the edge of the woods. He saw the people leaving one and going to the one he had shot at earlier. He dared not risk a shot at them, although he was in the mood to do so.

He made his way back to where he had taken the shots earlier. The descending darkness gave him more cover now, and he moved closer to the house in the hope of getting another shot at the woman who had murdered his brother.

He found a good spot and lay prone, getting into the firing position. He was a lot less nervous than earlier. The view in the eyepiece was much steadier. In the house's light, he could see the old man in his chair and two other men. They seemed to be talking animatedly.

Be patient, John, be patient.

The people from the other house were almost at their destination. This could be his chance. He settled down and looked through the gunsight with his finger on the trigger. He was steady.

He saw two women enter the room, one of them clutching her arm. Neither was Sienna Kraxler.

Be patient, John, be patient, he thought again. *Any second now.*

John trained the gun on the entrance to the room through which the two women had entered, convinced that Sienna would be next. He increased the pressure on the trigger. He played a game while he waited, putting the women alternately in the crosshairs.

The shot surprised everyone in the village of Oakwood, except the man pulling the trigger.

84

Victor's party heard the shot from the woods and sprinted for the house. Victor hit the door and stumbled in. The others followed with slightly more dignity.

"Come in. Again, why don't you?" said the old man.

"Where is Sienna? Is anyone hurt?" Victor addressed the room.

"No more than when you left. Less so than when you left," said the old man.

"What do you mean?" asked Victor.

"There is one less gunshot victim in the house," said the old man.

Victor ran around the corner to the stairwell and then straight back to the gathered company.

"Where is he?" Victor demanded.

"He had a second gun," Mike said.

"Shit!" Victor almost spat the word. "And you just let him go?"

"It was the sensible option," Cody said.

"So now we have two gunmen out there wishing us harm," Victor said.

"Or maybe one," Cody said. "One of them just shot the other, I think."

The room considered this.

"Still, one armed man wishing us harm."

Athena suddenly laughed.

"What?" demanded Victor.

"Sorry. My sick brain just conjured up the image of a one-armed man."

Victor sighed.

The door was thrown open, and Floyd fell into the house. He was barely conscious as he lay on his back.

Carlos recoiled from the prostrate figure. It was the figure from his recurring dream. He knew who it was and what he had done. Carlos was the only one in the room moving. He continued to move slowly backwards. Then he stopped, reversed course and launched a vicious kick into Floyd's ribs. Then another.

Victor rushed forward and pulled his brother away.

"No, Carlos! We need the story first." Victor said.

Carlos calmed. Both the Atkar men knelt beside Floyd, who tried to speak. It was almost inaudible.

"It was not all business. Not with your parents. I have often had pleasure when I should have just been doing business."

Floyd was white as a sheet now. Blood was still flowing from his leg wounds.

"What happened out in the woods?" Victor asked.

"No more guns out there. Sienna, safe." Floyd breathed.

Victor and Carlos just looked at each other.

Floyd looked at them in turn, "Just business this time. Sienna Kraxler is safe. Not back to the city, though. You take her back to the city for me. My last job." Floyd whispered.

Floyd's eyes darted back and forth. Unfocused.

"Sorry," Floyd managed. It was not entirely clear what he was apologising for, and it would never become clear. His eyes closed.

Carlos and Victor stood, looking down at the expired Floyd.

Carlos kicked him again.

So did Victor.

Then, together, they dragged the body outside and left it to any scavenging animals to dispose of.

85

Dawn broke on a crowded house. With the exception of Carlos, no one had slept very well. Carlos had slept dreamlessly for the first time since he had left Oakwood as a boy.

Victor knocked on the bedroom door.

"How are the wounded?"

Isabella said, "I'm fine. I'm not sure Sienna is up to walking back to the city, though."

"Maybe in a day or two." Sienna smiled from her bed.

Myra just smiled a weary smile at him.

"It's not over. Kelvin might not be in charge here, but he can do pretty much what he wants in the city," Myra said.

"So we should all stay here with Sienna for a few more days. Maybe we should use both houses, though." Victor smiled.

Over breakfast, Connie was engrossed in her MFB.

"Bad manners," scolded her mother.

"I have an idea."

"Do tell," suggested Sienna.

"This MFB is all rigged up as a Kraxler device. Remember, we all got one just before they were made illegal. Only a member of the Kraxler family can use a Kraxler MFB. It can tell from your sweat or something. I can't remember the details, but only a Kraxler can use it," Connie said.

"And your point is?" Myra asked.

"My point is that they are all linked. We can all access each other's MFBs."

"Again, your point is?"

"They record stuff happening around them."

"Again, your poi—."

"My point is that there was one in Dad's office. In the office where he is supposed to have killed Samantha," Connie explained.

"And?" Victor asked this time.

"And... So we can access what happened in Dad's office on the day all the grain in the barn turned to rat shit."

"That's some metaphor!" Victor exclaimed.

"We can copy it, send it to the authorities, and get him arrested," Connie explained.

"The same authorities that locked me up on the word of Kelvin Kraxler? He controls them, or at the very least has great influence with them."

Sienna was sitting up in bed now.

"Victor, there is a way," Sienna said.

They all looked at her.

"Feeling better, are we?" Isabella commented.

"If we can transfer the recording from the MFB in the Kraxler building to the one Connie has here. We can send a copy to Elliott. Elliott should be told all this," Sienna said.

"At the moment, he believes everything Kelvin says to him," Myra said.

"No, idiots," Connie said.

"We get the recording here to check it out for ourselves. Once we have confirmed the content—"

"You don't believe me?" Sienna said.

"Of course I believe you! Once we have confirmed the

content is available and definitively incriminating, we should be able to send the evidence to everyone who has an MFB in the city. That will include everyone with money or power, and will definitely include Elliott. The head of the Kraxler family will be well and truly fucked," Connie said.

Isabella cleared her throat. A clear indication that she thought such language from her granddaughter was unladylike.

"Sorry," Connie said, "but it could work."

"Can you get the recorded stuff visible to us all?" Victor asked

"Yep. No problem. Can you give Sienna and I maybe thirty minutes to find it?" Connie said.

"Time for you to make breakfast if the old man has anything left. I will come down so that we can all see it together. Everyone should see it. See him for what he really was! Is!" There was a tremor in Sienna's voice, and it had nothing to do with weakness after her injury. It indicated an inner anger and an inner strength to all in the room.

Forty-five minutes later, the downstairs room of the old man's cottage was once again packed with people.

"Connie. Show them all," Sienna said.

"This shows you the real man that you all work for and the man we all loved and respected. It reveals a dark side to a man with great power. A dark side to a man with no respect for family or friends, let alone colleagues in business," Connie said.

A second later, the MFB showed a holographic display of the events surrounding Sam's murder in Kelvin's office.

Myra had become very pale. Even though she already knew the story and had believed it, watching and listening to the recording of the event sickened her. She left the house to throw up. Isabella was a boiling pot of silent fury.

Myra returned. "Send it to everyone except Kelvin. Make sure Elliott gets a copy first."

Silence filled the room.

The old man spoke up. "It might be an entertaining end for a vicious, selfish, cruel Kraxler. I wonder if Kelvin's MFB will record the receipt of this recording and the visit of Elliott Keogh. I would like to see that."

"I never want to see him again, on one of these things or in the flesh," Myra said.

"You owe me. You all owe me," said the old man. "I want paying."

"Debts will be paid," said Athena and Miklos in unison.

"You can pay mine now," said the old man.

"What is it you want?" Victor asked.

"I want to be the one. The one who sends the message that will bring down Kelvin Kraxler."

"You can't," Connie said.

"Set it up so that I can press a button or whatever."

"You can't. It won't work for you. It has to be a family member. I expla—"

"Let's try. Debts must be paid."

"Try," Victor said. "This whole village is gone because of Kelvin Kraxler. Let him try."

"It won't—"

"Let him try!" Victor said.

Connie did stuff to the MFB for a few seconds and did not argue with Victor.

"Here. It won't work for you. I'm telling you, it won't work, but try if you must. Press firmly anywhere on the thing with both thumbs."

The old man took the MFB and pressed as instructed. The machine audibly vibrated slightly.

Connie snatched it back from the old man and looked at it in puzzlement.

"It's sent! It shouldn't have sent, but it's sent!" Connie exclaimed.

Connie looked up from the machine in her hand and into the face of the old man. No one spoke.

"Good," said the old man.

Connie hadn't taken her eyes off him. He smiled at her.

Connie opened her mouth to speak, but no words came. The old man smiled again.

Connie tried again," You're a—"

"Kraxler." Interrupted the old man. "I have the misfortune to be the cause of all this. I am Ivan Kraxler. Kelvin's father. By sending that recording out, I feel that I have at least begun to pay some of my debt, and debts must be paid."

The silence in the room was complete.

Ivan broke it, "You all have business to attend to in the city. Once you have all had breakfast and recovered your strength, I think you should leave me to my village."

86

Elliott received the recording of his wife's murder about an hour before the so-called authorities in the city received it. Before Kelvin received it.

He walked slowly into the Kraxler building and spoke politely to the door guard.

"Mr Kraxler in?"

The guard nodded, and Elliott took the elevator to Kelvin's office. He went in without knocking.

"Elliott. Thank goodness someone is around. I can't get hold of anyone. Elliott, are you okay?"

"I'm fine, Kelvin. Just needed to check something before I start my day," Elliott said.

Kelvin was looking out at the city below with his back to Elliott.

"What is it you need to check? Nobody is around, and there is some serious stuff we need to sort out." Kelvin said, still looking out the window.

He turned to find Elliott pushing on the furniture.

"Elliott. What the hell are you doing?" Kelvin demanded.

"Checking."

Elliott continued pushing at the large sofa, which moved

back a couple of feet. He looked down, paused, and then, without a word, headed for the door.

"Elliott? Elliott?"

Kelvin looked down at the floor. The floor that had been covered by the sofa. There, glistening amongst the dust, was a single earring. Sam's earring.

87

It was early evening when Victor walked into The Straight Banana bar. It looked upmarket. It was probably expensive, but he didn't mind. He took a stool at the bar and waited.

"Vic! About time! What can I get you?" Athena's face beamed at him.

"The Straight Banana! Where did that come from, A?

"I had to keep a fruity reference in the name, and it had to be a bit off the wall. I mean, The Orange Room had no orange in it at all," she said as she poured him his usual.

"This place going well?"

"Different clientele to the last place. Riverside. Upmarket. An exception will be made for you as you are part owner."

"You get enough upmarket customers in to make us a profit?" Victor asked.

"Well, I supplement the upmarket with some local dockland flavour. There are some local characters who I sell the booze to cheaply, but they buy a lot of it. The upmarket customers flock in to see the local riff-raff and to feel superior. Win, win." Athena said.

"It's quiet at the moment."

"Give it an hour or so, and the place will be half full of

Miklos's sailors. Isabella is paying him to teach a load of no-hopers to sail her old wooden boats for her, as fuel is so expensive now. My god, he drinks like a fish, but at least he pays. That useless bastard Mason has tried to come in here sponging off the sailors. They won't have it, and I won't have it.

Victor smiled.

"You got somewhere quiet?" Victor asked.

"Never thought you'd ask. We have rooms," she said.

"A. Stop it."

She sighed.

"Just a booth for two. I have a meeting."

She nodded and guided him to a corner booth overlooking the entrance.

"Will this be satisfactory for sir?"

"Thanks, A," he said.

A few moments later, a youngish man approached and slid into the booth opposite Victor.

"You good, Vic?"

"Buzzing, just buzzing, Mr Moyes."

"Good to see you." Victor raised a hand to attract Athena's attention.

"Good to see you too, Vic."

"So, tell me. Did you jump, or were you rescued?"

"I hated cabbage as a child. A whole day languishing in rotten cabbage has not changed my mind. They found me, Vic. Spotted on a drone feed. Then they rescued me."

"And you are back at Vantuba prison?"

"They have repaired the place, but guarding that rabble after what happened has proved an unpopular career choice. We have new guards now, and I am the governor."

"Tell me you get out of your office now and again."

"I do my rounds last thing, as when you were there. I like

my routine and have added to it a little."

"Oh?"

"I take a notable inmate on a guided tour of the kitchens each evening. He gets shown the garbage chute. He gets offered the garbage chute. Then he goes back to his cell. It is slightly cruel, I know."

"Cruelty comes in varying degrees." Victor smiled. "Does he get many visitors?"

"His son comes occasionally, but not often," Luc said.

"I think Leon is working with Cody now. So is the Medic. Most of my debts have been repaid, but I still owe Medic Mike."

"Still illegal stuff, I expect."

"Someone has to do it. And I suppose it's better that we know who we are working with," Victor said.

"And what about the rest of the Kraxler family?" Luc asked.

"Isabella is not taking it easy. She runs a nice little enterprise shipping stuff up and down the river under sail. There is no fuel but Mother Nature. Her only problem is dealing with Miklos. He is almost too delighted to be back on the water and in places like this. Connie has gone back to her farm and her hiking obsession, but comes back to the city much more often now."

"And Myra Kraxler?"

"Spends most of her time helping Sienna sort out a luxury apartment. A ground floor luxury apartment."

"And your brother?"

He spends most of his time in Oakwood. He and Ivan Kraxler are working to get people back to the village. The old man is fading a little, but is hanging in there. The two have become oddly close. Carlos comes back to visit us all quite often, though. He, like me, is now the part owner of a drinking establishment, too."

"Fanny's and Dick's?"

"Exactly right."

"So, who's running the Kraxler empire?"

"Elliott. He was deeply involved in the legitimate part of the business before Sam was murdered. We both think Kelvin is running at least part of the organisation, from his cell."

"Not sure how he is doing that."

"No, but it feels like he is. Hopefully, his influence will wane. Too many people want to be rid of him."

"It's not just up to people, though, is it? He seems to have ways," Luc said.

"You and I need to keep watch for any Kraxler resurgence."

"Agreed."

"And what about you, Vic? What are you up to?"

"Helping Elliott and generally clearing up the mess of the last few years."

"And that fills your time?" Luc asked with a smile.

"Well, I am also spending quite a lot of time sorting out a luxury apartment. A ground floor luxury apartment." Victor smiled a beaming smile at his old captor.

"The same luxury apartment?"

"The same," Victor said, still beaming at the thought.

"Vic, I have something for you. I should have given it to you sooner, but…"

"What?"

Luc reached into his pocket and brought his closed hand to the tabletop. He opened his palm in front of Victor.

"No! My Father's compass!"

A small tear ran down Victor's smiling face.

"You good, Vic?"

"Buzzing, Mr Moyes. Just buzzing."

Reviews

If you enjoyed this book, please consider leaving a review. Just scan the QR code to get to the review page.

daijoneswriting@gmail.com

Acknowledgements

There are a great number of people to thank for their help in the creation of this book. My wife and my sons have been constant sources of encouragement and support throughout. Jessica Lawrence has supplied editorial skills, and a whole Tribe of like-minded people piled on the help and encouragement needed to get the book finished.

daijoneswriting@gmail.com

Printed in Dunstable, United Kingdom

77920813R00173